STIRLING COUNCIL LIBRARIES

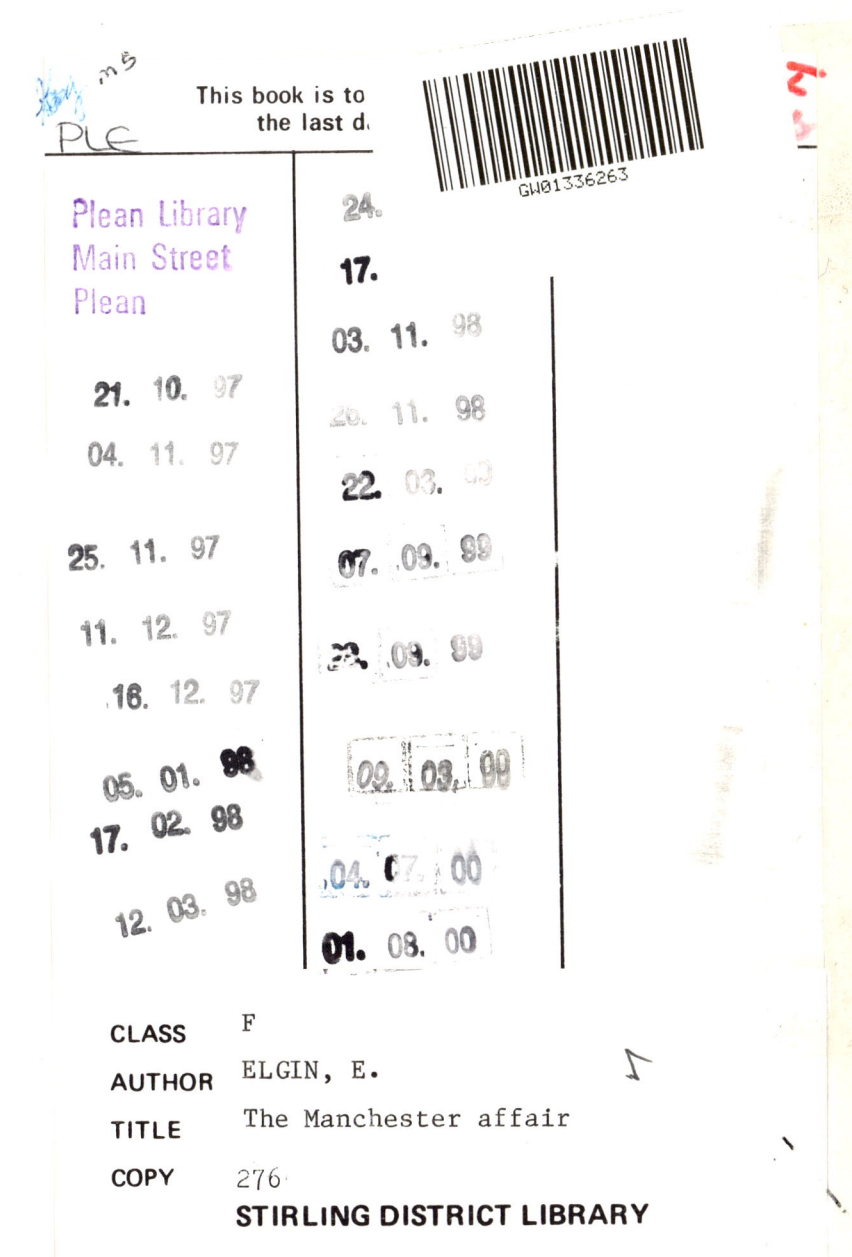

3 8048 00521 1276

This book is to
the last d

GW01336263

Plean Library
Main Street
Plean

24.
17.
03. 11. 98
20. 11. 98
22. 03. 99
07. 09. 99
22. 09. 99
09. 03. 00
04. 07. 00
01. 08. 00

21. 10. 97
04. 11. 97
25. 11. 97
11. 12. 97
16. 12. 97
05. 01. 98
17. 02. 98
12. 03. 98

CLASS	F
AUTHOR	ELGIN, E.
TITLE	The Manchester affair
COPY	276

STIRLING DISTRICT LIBRARY

The Manchester Affair

By the same author

The House In Abercromby Square
The Manchester Affair
Shadow of Dark Water
Mistress of Luke's Folly
Whistle in the Dark
The Rose Hedge

The Manchester Affair

Elizabeth Elgin

ROBERT HALE · LONDON

© Elizabeth Elgin 1977
First published in Great Britain 1977
This edition 1997

ISBN 0 7090 6128 5

Robert Hale Limited
Clerkenwell House
Clerkenwell Green
London EC1R 0HT

The right of Elizabeth Elgin to be identified
as author of this work has been asserted by her
in accordance with the Copyright, Designs
and Patents Act 1988.

2 4 6 8 10 9 7 5 3 1

00521 1276

Printed in Great Britain by
St Edmundsbury Press Limited, Bury St Edmunds, Suffolk.
Bound by WBC Book Manufacturers Limited
Bridgend, Mid Glamorgan.

ONE

Rachel Parker sat in the summer-room at Fair Oaks and looked out towards the farthest edge of their garden, watching her husband's methodical pacing of his boundaries, noticing the movements of his head, knowing he was making mental notes to be passed on before he left for Rotterdam.

Almost instinctively, Rachel shrank into the quiet of her surroundings. She sat there often—mostly when she was troubled or when John's restless personality seemed to overpower her. It was the one room in their large, luxurious house that seemed truly her own. John called it a conservatory, but to Rachel, with its white-tiled floor and iron furniture, it was a summer-room, a place of perpetual greenness where vines climbed the rough stone walls and glossy-leaved plants stood tall and lush, tangling with trailing fairylike ferns. It helped to still the turbulence that seemed always now to be gnawing inside her, understanding her fears, reaching out gently to wrap its green-cool calm protectively around her.

This time tomorrow, she thought dispassionately, John would be gone and before he went, before he left his possessions behind him, he was making a final check as he always did. And Anne and me, we are his possessions, too, Rachel acknowledged. We are protected and indulged and we lack nothing, yet I would gladly change all this for the little house in Manchester. But

Manchester belonged to a faraway life and John's mouth set itself trap-like whenever she mentioned it, so she never talked about the old days any more.

Rachel started guiltily as her husband turned abruptly and walked towards the house. It was almost as if he had beamed-in on her thoughts and read her mind. But that was impossible because they weren't all that close these days she thought with a little surge of pain. She could recall quite clearly the last time they made love because it had been when Anne and Graham announced their engagement, two months ago—the night of her forty-fifth birthday. Almost always now, John was too preoccupied, too bound up with tomorrow's business to notice her silent need.

Once, in the old days, when John came home to her after a particularly long haul, she had known how to unwind the coiled springs of ambition inside him; a hot bath, a clean shift and a can of cold lager. And after that, if there was tension in him still, she would take his face between her hands and touch his mouth gently with her lips, kissing him lightly, insistently, without speaking; kissing him until the tenseness was gone and frustration forgotten. Then she would place her lips close to his cheek and murmur,

'Love me, John. Love me...'

She would say it softly and sensuously so that the words were only a gentle moving of her lips and her asking little more than a breath in his ear.

All that was part of the Manchester-time, the far-off days when she had ached for the feel of his child inside her, when they had not known that John would never have the son he longed for or that the fault would lie with herself.

Abruptly Rachel shut out the past and picking up the notebook that lay beside her began to count the names she had written in it as she heard John's footsteps on the gravel path outside.

'The garden's looking well, Rachel. You might mention it to Bob.'

'Seventy. Seventy-two, seventy-four,' Rachel replied without lifting her eyes.

Yes, she conceded, just like the garden, everything about them looked well and serene and prosperous. They had built this, their dream-house, far away from the city on an acre of meadow land and the architect had left untouched the two fine oak trees that grew on it. So they called the place Fair Oaks and an old man called Bob worked in its garden whenever his aching joints allowed.

'More lists?'

John flicked his lighter as if he didn't expect a reply.

'Mm, and it's getting out of hand. Over a hundred names already. It reads more like one of your business dinners than the guest-list for Anne's wedding.'

'So? Pleasure and business—who's complaining?'

He drew deeply on his cigarette. Anyone would think that Rachel didn't want Anne to marry young Graham which was a bit stupid when anybody could see it would be the making of the girl, he brooded silently. Rachel had spoiled their daughter. She had overdone the *you-were-something-special* bit, in his considered opinion. Anne should have been treated like any other kid, adopted or not. John liked Graham Hobson and the fact that the boy's father was also in the haulage business pleased him. The marriage could do nothing but good, he pondered, bring the two companies closer. It could even bring them together, one day. They would be powerful, then; something to be reckoned with!

'Anyway,' John urged when Rachel remained irritatingly silent, 'it'll be a good marriage. Young Graham will end up in Hobson's boardroom eventually and we've practically watched him grow up—know all about his background...'

'Oh yes, John,' Rachel flung. 'It won't so much be losing a daughter as gaining a foothold in Hobson's Transport!'

She was sorry as soon as she had said the words, but John's remark about Graham's background irked her, the more so when it emphasized how little they knew about Anne's.

The panicky sadness welled up inside her as it always did when she thought too deeply of the coming wedding. She was going to miss Anne desperately. The house would be lonelier than ever. She saw so little of John these days and even when he was at home, half of him was still with Parker's Haulage. She and John were drawing apart again and almost always Anne seemed to stand at the centre of that withdrawing. In spite of all the love their daughter had been given, something was lacking. True, Anne was an adopted child but it hadn't made any difference to their love for her, Rachel reasoned. She had never failed to reassure her, tell her how wanted she had been, how she had looked, that day they got her, as if she had been made specially for them.

But despite all her efforts, Rachel knew that Anne was growing away from them. She had drawn a barrier around herself, strangely intangible yet impenetrable as steel. At first, her moods were dismissed as teenage truculence, for it was shortly before Anne's fourteenth birthday that Rachel had finally been forced to acknowledge that all was not right.

'She'll get over it,' she whispered fiercely, again and again.

But Anne became more silent and more secretive with the passing of the months and soon even the briefest glimpse of the carefree child she had been was a rarity. Could John be right, Rachel wondered. Would marriage be good for Anne? There was no doubting Graham's love for her and he was a nice young man—easy-going and uncomplicated—Anne's absolute opposite, in fact.

Rachel snapped shut her notebook. She didn't know why she was worrying so. After all, she reasoned, the wedding wasn't until September—a good three months away and the essential arrangements were going smoothly. But then, John was well on his way to becoming a rich man and money was a great smoother.

Had it all been worth it, Rachel thought. Wouldn't they have been happier with their one lorry and the tiny terraced house in Manchester? Sometimes she was almost sure that even yet John was restless for the feel and smell of a lorry cab; that being John Parker of Parker's Haulage hadn't quite given him the satisfaction he imagined it would during those far-off weary days behind the wheel and the cold nights on lonely roads.

'Hey there!'

Dimly she heard John's voice and focused her eyes on the fingers that snapped under her nose.

'You were miles away, Rachel. What were you thinking about?'

She raised her head and looked steadily into her husband's eyes.

'Only wondering if you are happy now, John—if it was worth it, all the struggling, the uprooting...'

'Coming down here, you mean? Building up the business? Getting us a place like this to live in? Of course it was worth it!'

He said it firmly as if leaving the little house in Manchester had meant nothing to him; that to give up their first home so deliberately was no more than one planned step nearer the riches he was determined to amass. So their furniture was piled on to his lorry and with Anne a baby of five weeks, they came to Birmingham and another little terraced house.

'The Midlands,' John had said. 'Heavy industry—that's where the money's to be got, Rachel. There'll be plenty of work for me there. That's where we'll make it!'

And they had made it. In no time at all, their one old lorry became part of a fleet. They got bigger and bigger. They were rich, now, and the getting of those riches had driven a wedge through their happiness.

'Where's Anne?' John asked, almost as an afterthought as he walked into the sitting-room.

'Out with Graham. They've gone to see his old aunt. I believe there's some family china she wants them to have.'

Rachel felt vaguely irritated. She didn't want to talk about Anne. Sometimes she didn't even want to think about her. Just to think made her uneasy. Deliberately changing the subject she said,

'I've laid out your clothes for Rotterdam on the bed in the spare room. Just check if there's anything I've missed, will you?'

'It'll be all right. You've packed for me before,' came

the brusque reply. 'Just so long as there's enough socks. I don't mind Miss Tremlitt rinsing out the odd shirt, but I draw the line at having to ask her to wash socks for me, Rachel.'

'There's enough socks for a month,' she murmured, disinterested.

Miss Tremlitt, Rachel mused. Did John's sedate secretary have another name? If she did, Rachel had never heard it used. As far back as she could remember, it had always been Miss Tremlitt. Maybe she should be glad that it was the faithful Miss T. who was going to Rotterdam with John and not some long-legged secretary-bird.

She hunched her shoulders into a gesture of resignation and trailed into the sitting-room after John. Would it matter all that much who went with him, the way their marriage seemed to be, now?

Mentally Rachel shook away the thought. **There wasn't a dolly-secretary, just Miss Tremlitt, whose life was divided equally between Parker's Haulage and a widowed mother who was a semi-invalid.** Rachel liked Miss Tremlitt. She had first come to work for John more than seventeen years ago—about the same time as the triumphant acquisition of his third lorry. She had been a Jill-of all-trades then and her office was in a converted corner of the lock-up yard John once rented.

'What will you do in Rotterdam?'

Rachel really tried to understand the workings of Parker's Haulage.

John was silent for a moment and she knew he was arranging his reply into the simplest possible language before making it.

'Well—briefly—empty vehicles are wasteful. Trucks are going to the Continent fully loaded and returning empty. I want to see about getting some return-loads. It's simple economics, isn't it?'

Rachel supposed it was.

'Who looks after Miss Tremlitt's mother when she goes away?'

'Some relative from up north, I believe.'

'Her sister from Manchester?'

John shrugged and without answering turned away from her and picked up his brief-case.

Rachel took the mild snub calmly. She should have remembered that Manchester was taboo, that John didn't like to be reminded of the old days.

'I'll make us some coffee.'

She usually made coffee when there didn't seem anything more to say or to do.

The phone purred as she filled the kettle. Absently she reached for the kitchen extension.

'Three-nine-six-one. Rachel Parker.'

'Good evening. Would it be possible for me to speak to Mr John Parker?'

'I'll get him. Who is it, please?'

'Duty-sergeant, madam. Birmingham City Police.'

'*The police?* What is it? What's wrong?'

Rachel's mouth went dry. Something had happened to Anne and Graham!

'If I could have a word with your husband, Mrs Parker,' the voice was gentle, yet firm, 'it might be better.'

Rachel covered the mouthpiece with a hand that was suddenly cold and clammy.

'It's the police, John,' she called huskily. 'They want *you!*'

The fear in her voice brought John quickly to her side.

'Here, give it to me. Likely it's only one of the drivers in a bit of trouble...'

No! urged Rachel's reason. It couldn't be a driver. The drivers knew to phone the depot, didn't they?

Heart bumping, she fixed her eyes on her husband's face.

'Parker here. What can I do for you?'

There was a small silence then a fresh surge of panic twisted itself into a knot in Rachel's throat as suddenly John's face drained itself of colour.

'Anne? You mean Anne Parker, my daughter? She's *where*?'

Anne? Oh, please, let her be all right? Rachel prayed silently.

'Yes—yes, I understand. I'll be down. About twenty minutes. Yes, of course. Thank you. Good night, sergeant.'

John's jaw was set tight and Rachel jumped as the receiver slammed down.

'She's all right, John? She's not hurt?'

'Oh yes, Rachel, Anne's all right!' The reply was harsh with sarcasm. 'She's being well taken care of. She's at a police station in Birmingham. They've arrested her—for shop-lifting!'

A cry of disbelief jerked from Rachel's throat.

'No! They've made a mistake. Anne's with Graham!'

'Anne's with the police and she's there because she got caught lifting cheap jewellery!'

Rachel swallowed hard. She had known, deep inside her, that something would happen. Anne's resentment had been simmering far too long. Sooner or later it had been bound to flare into open rebellion. Once again she felt the all too familiar gnawing inside her and an invisible finger trickled cold fear down her back. That fear was for Anne and the fact that she, Anne's mother, seemed helpless to do anything about it.

'Are you coming with me, Rachel?'

John's eyes were cold and angry.

'Oh—to the police station? Yes John. Yes ... of course ...'

Her voice sounded alien, as if she had no part in what was happening. She felt a terrible aloneness, an inexplicable terror and only one thing was certain in the confusion of her mind. The phone-call they had just received was only the start of things. She knew it without the shadow of a doubt.

She started as she heard the banging-open of the garage doors. She didn't want to go. She knew that what she had secretly dreaded for so long was about to begin, yet, despite the woman's instinct that screamed *No!* inside her she called.

'I'm coming, John. Wait for me, please?'

Realizing he couldn't beat the amber light, John trod heavily on the brake and brought his car to a halt at the intersection.

Rachel let go her indrawn breath then said,

'Look—let's not collect a ticket for speeding. We're in a thirty ...'

They had driven towards Birmingham without speaking and the words rushed out as if a safety-valve inside her had blown.

'I know where we are,' John snapped, 'but I'm damned angry!'

He shifted his position and glared up at the red light,

willing it to change as impatiently he tapped his fingers on the wheel.

'There's a nasty streak in that girl, Rachel. You've spoiled her silly and now look what's happened!'

'*A nasty streak?* What do you mean?' Rachel flung round to face her husband. 'It's our daughter you're talking about, John!'

'Yes, and I'm reminding you that this isn't the first time she's been in trouble, so don't go on at me. I'm just the poor mug who gets her out of it!'

John Parker's eyes narrowed angrily.

'Anne's getting married soon, remember? What if this lot gets into the papers, Rachel? Do you realize what a mess she's got herself into this time?'

The car lurched forward, responding to the impatient pressure of his feet. Rachel wound up her window. The people in the car alongside them at the lights had listened to every angry word. They had looked guiltily away as she turned suddenly. And that was what it would be like from now on, Rachel thought bitterly. Anne had been accused of shop-lifting and they would have to get used to the turning-away, the embarrassed dropping of eyes.

But who was thinking about Anne and her feelings? Rachel's heart went out to her daughter. Somewhere she once read that shop-lifting was often a cry from the heart, a plea for help. Was Anne asking for help? Had the other trouble been a part of it, too? Rachel thought back to the time of the first incident. Oh, John had managed to smooth it over very quietly. John was always good at fixing things.

Anne had been caught stealing from her schoolfriends; near-worthless things and trifling sums of money, all placed neatly in a little box in her desk for anyone to discover. Anne Parker didn't need to steal; that fact in itself was sufficient for her headmistress to let her off with a strongly-worded caution and they had been able to breathe easily again.

'Well, Rachel? *Do* you realize the mess we're in?'

John's voice cut into her thoughts.

'Oh, John. Let's not be angry. Please don't let's say anything we'll be sorry for? Can't we wait and see what Anne has to say, first?'

Her voice trembled with tears and sensing her distress, John clenched his hands on the wheel until his knuckles showed white.

'I'm sorry,' he replied, his voice clipped. 'It's just that it's going to be one heck of a job getting her out of *this* one!'

Tacitly they lapsed into silence again. John was right, Rachel knew it. This time they were dealing with the police. This time it wasn't petty-pilfering from blazer-pockets or even, more seriously, a vicious attack on a classmate.

Rachel closed her eyes at the memory of that girl's face, bruised and bloodied by Anne's angry hands. They were never able to find what triggered-off such white-hot rage. They had just been relieved to sweep the whole thing under the mat when the parents of the injured girl reluctantly agreed not to take the matter further.

Oh, Anne, Rachel whispered inside her. Where did it go wrong? I love you so much. You have always been *my* Anne, right from that first day we got you. And it didn't matter one bit that you weren't nurtured in my body and that I didn't know the pangs of your birth, because you were the child of my heart's yearning. Did you sense, even when we got you, that perhaps I paid too dearly for you? Did you understand that to get you I had to fight like a pagan, set my marriage at risk so that I might hold a child—any woman's child—in my arms?

A tear fell on to Rachel's clenched hands and she let it lay there. They hadn't far to go now, she thought with dull, thudding fear. Soon, they would know.

Rachel knew she would always remember that police station; the blue-painted doors, the off-white walls, the floor tiles. Especially she would remember the floor tiles. They were the same mottled white as those in the summer-room at Fair Oaks and it didn't seem right.

In a stiff voice John gave his name to the sergeant at the counter-like desk. He seemed a pleasant man, Rachel thought, wondering if he had a daughter, too, and if she sometimes caused him to worry.

Cell three.

Dimly Rachel heard the words and as she grasped their implication she felt the colour leave her face. Turning to John she saw the same disbelief mirrored in his eyes.

'My daughter—locked up?' he demanded. 'Surely there's been a mistake? I think I'd like to get hold of my solicitor.'

'By all means, sir,' the sergeant nodded, 'but it can't do a lot of good—not at this stage. Your daughter's been charged already, you see. It's just a question of bail, now. We're perfectly willing to grant bail.'

'What do you mean—*bail*?'

He could not disguise the anger in his voice.

'Look sir, it's not my case,' the sergeant replied quietly. 'W.P.C. Wareing will be with you in a minute. She'll tell you all about it.'

Rachel felt a sob of panic rising in her throat. It was all a nightmare, she thought wildly, and it was happening to *them*!

'Mr and Mrs Parker? I'm W.P.C. Wareing.'

As one, Rachel and John jerked round. The woman constable who stood there smiled at them kindly.

'Would you like to see your daughter now, or is there anything you would like to ask me first?'

'I understand she's been charged,' John said, stiffly. 'Surely we had a right to be here, officer? Couldn't it have waited?'

'There was no point, Mr Parker,' came the mild reply. 'Your daughter made a statement in which she pleaded guilty to the charge. She's an adult, you know. She gave her age as nineteen.'

'But locked up—like a criminal ...'

'Shop-lifting is a criminal offence, sir, but you'll be able to take your daughter home with you, just as soon as bail has been settled.'

'Then does that mean she'll have to go to court?' Rachel gasped.

'Yes, I'm afraid it does. But that shouldn't be for a little while. We have to establish that this is your daughter's first offence and see the Social Worker's report, maybe.'

The young woman was trying to be kind, Rachel realized, but for all that she said dully,

'Anne couldn't go to prison ... ?'

'I really don't know about that, Mrs Parker, but with a first offence, the Magistrates are sometimes lenient.'

But was it a first offence? What about the trouble at school? Would all that come out now, Rachel wondered, a feeling of nausea washing over her. Despairingly she turned to John for comfort but there was only suppressed outrage in his face that seemed at any moment to be capable of bursting from him in violent anger.

'You can see your daughter now, if you'll come with me?'

There were three doors on either side of the narrow passage down which they walked, each of them fitted with a small, circular hole and a square flap-like structure. Rachel knew exactly what they were for. The little round window was a peep-hole and they pushed food-plates through the flap. She knew it as part of a fantasy world; make-believe on a television screen. Now it was desperately real. It was happening to their daughter and neither the desk-sergeant nor W.P.C. Wareing were actors.

The cell door clicked open.

'Here's your mother and father, Anne.'

For a moment they stood there, looking with fascinated horror at the bench-bed built against one wall and the half-screened lavatory in the corner. There was no privacy. They would be able to see that lavatory through the peep-hole, Rachel thought with cold shock. Then gradually she forced herself to look at the figure sitting on the bench; a girl wearing jeans and a smock-top and flat, scuffed sandals. Her chin rested on her hands and her long, red-gold hair hung loose over her face.

Rachel ran her tongue round her lips then said,

'Anne? It's all right, now. We've come to take you home, just as soon as Dad's seen to the—'

Bail. She couldn't say the word.

Gently she laid an arm round her daughter's shoulders but the tears she expected did not come and Rachel felt instead a stiffening of Anne's body, a drawing-away, a pulling round of the barrier again. She wanted to talk to her daughter, to comfort her, but not in this alien place, she thought. And anyway, maybe she wasn't even allowed to?

Suddenly Rachel wanted to take Anne away. Maybe at home, the tight-faced stranger might become her beloved daughter once more.

'Can we see the Inspector now?' she whispered.

The constable nodded, unspeaking, and as they left the small, bare room Rachel turned to smile at the forlorn little figure but there was no response and it seemed she could have been looking at some other woman's daughter.

Some other woman's daughter? Oh, but that was a laugh, she thought bitterly, if you liked sick jokes.

The familiar pain of fear gnawed afresh inside her. Where would it all end, she thought wildly as the door clashed shut behind them.

TWO

The garage doors at Fair Oaks were wide open, just as they had left them two hours ago; just as the police said you should never leave your garage doors. But they were home now and perhaps someone would speak, Rachel thought, remembering the awful silence of the drive back.

John stopped the car outside the front door. For the first time in half an hour he spoke.

'You go on in. I'm going up to the golf club.'

'The golf club?' Rachel gasped. 'You're going *out*?'

'Go into the house, Anne,' John interrupted, tersely indicating that what he had to say was not for his daughter's hearing.

'*The golf club?*' Rachel flung into the attack again as soon as they were alone. 'I don't understand you John. I just don't understand!'

'Then it won't be any use my trying to explain that I'm going to see Marcus James, will it?'

'But do you have to? We've got to talk. Can't it wait until Monday?'

Marcus James was their friend. He was also a very hard-working solicitor. John had no right to interrupt his Saturday night at the club, Rachel reasoned.

'Yes Rachel, I *do* have to and no, it *won't* wait until Monday. I'm due in Rotterdam tomorrow evening, or had you forgotten?'

'You're still going? You're actually going away with all this hanging over us?'

'Why not? For one thing I've got two appointments lined up for Monday morning and that's only the start of it. Do you expect me to cancel them at this late hour? What would I say, Rachel? "Our daughter has been charged with shop-lifting so I can't make it." Anyway,' he shrugged, 'I'll be back before it gets into court, won't I?'

'Will you, John?'

Rachel's lips were so stiff with shock that she could hardly speak.

'Of course I will, and meantime Marcus can see to things better than I can. With me out of the way it'll be better and you know it, otherwise I might be tempted to give that young madam what she deserves!'

'What do you mean, John?'

Rachel's voice was low and challenging. She knew exactly what her husband meant but she wanted to hear him say it. Defiantly she tilted her head, daring him with her eyes to answer her.

'I mean that I just might slap her bottom, grown-up though she may be!' he flung. 'And what's more, I should have done it years ago!'

Rachel clenched her hands tightly. With all the self-control she could summon she swung her legs out of the car then closed the door with a deliberate quiet.

'I won't wait up for you,' she said, her voice rough with suppressed outrage. 'Don't waken me when you come to bed.'

She walked into the house without looking back. Her whole body shook. She had wanted to strike out, to clench her fist and slam it blindly into her husband's uncaring face.

'Don't waken me up,' she had said. Oh, how stupid to think that perhaps tonight—because they would be apart for two weeks—that just tonight, John might have remembered she was still his wife.

Anne was in the sitting-room when Rachel found her, curled up into a tight little ball in the corner of the settee. She tilted her head, her eyes troubled yet aloof. Wearily Rachel sank down beside her, all anger spent, her head throbbing with mental fatigue. She did not attempt to reach out for Anne. She dare not risk another rebuff.

'*Why*, darling?' she whispered. 'Please tell me? I want to understand, truly I do.'

There was a small silence then Anne said,

'I don't know why. I just did it, that's all.'

She said it without remorse and her words pierced Rachel's heart like small, sharp knife-thrusts. Then rising to her feet she walked towards the door.

'I'm going to bed. Best not be around when Dad gets back.'

For a second she hesitated then half turned.

Hopefully Rachel lifted her head, not daring to speak.

'By the way, mother,' Anne's chin tilted defiantly. 'The wedding's off. Just thought I'd let you know.'

She said it flippantly as if it were of little consequence, then closed the door behind her with a finality that defied Rachel to follow her.

For a moment Rachel sat stiff with shock, her world reeling about her. Until now, life had been like a pond, beautiful and outwardly calm and all the disturbing things just half-sensed ripples beneath its surface. But today Anne had stolen a heart-shaped locket set with imitation turquoise and the little bauble had splashed and crashed into that pond with the force of a great destructive boulder.

Despairingly Rachel closed her eyes, then with the instinct of a homing bird, made blindly for the summer-room. It closed its green peace around her at once and she sank gratefully on to the white iron bench. Breathing deeply she looked through the open doors to where a blackbird piped from a blossom-covered cherry branch and the May dusk gentled the outlines of the oak trees. Forget-me-nots frothed dimly blue amongst sweet-smelling wallflowers and in the distance the evening hills rolled purple. But the beauty was lost upon Rachel, for Anne, the daughter she loved with all her heart had shut her out and John had left her when she desperately needed him beside her. Not for one moment, she thought, had it occurred to him to postpone his trip to Rotterdam, for nothing seemed to matter now but Parker's Haulage. Not Anne, she thought bitterly, nor me.

She gave a little shiver as she remembered the last time they came almost to breaking-point. It had been long ago, during the Manchester-time. Once, they were so in love, so close. Their life together had been near-perfect until the day they knew for certain there could never be children.

'All right, sweetheart,' John comforted. 'It's not the end of the world. We've still got each other.'

For a time they clung even more closely, each determined to comfort the other and it helped make the pain of knowing less acute. Then Rachel suggested they try to adopt a child and with that innocent, hopeful suggestion came the first split in their oneness. John's reply had been violent and uncompromising.

'No, Rachel, I won't do it! I couldn't take some other man's son—not even for you,' he jerked, his face taut and white.

He flung himself into his work with renewed aggression, then, and all her pleading, her tears and finally her open hostility had failed to move him.

'*No adoption*, Rachel!'

From then on their marriage trembled. Soon, the most innocent remark seemed ripe for misunderstanding, their brief conversations clipped and bitter. John's long hauls with his lorry became more frequent and Rachel had come to know desperate fear. Fear for John, for herself, for their marriage. Then suddenly, when her heart was close to breaking, when she thought she could not take one more night sharing the bed of a stranger, it was John who surrendered.

'Rachel?' he whispered forlornly into the darkness, 'Forgive me? We'll adopt a baby ...'

She reached out for him then across the great divide that had been so long between them and the bitter months were wiped out by a coming together that was tearful and urgent.

Six months later they had adopted Anne. Rachel was glad for John's sake that they were given a little girl. She wouldn't have wanted him to take another man's son.

Desperately Rachel jerked her thoughts away from the past. The present mattered now, because it was beginning to happen all over again. She recognized the signs and this time there would be no second chances for them, no coming together she thought with a shudder of dread, because neither of them seemed to care enough any more.

'Mrs Parker?'

The words were gently spoken yet they made Rachel start.

'Graham? Oh, it's you—'

She looked up into the troubled brown eyes of Anne's fiancé and smiled a welcome.

'Sit down and talk to me. I'm in need of company tonight. Or is it Anne you've come to see? She's gone to bed, but I'll call her—'

'No, please don't. It *is* you I want to talk to. I've heard about what happened today. I want to help.'

'You've heard, Graham?' Rachel gasped. '*Already?*'

'From Anne's father. I met him as he was turning out of the gate. He's just told me.'

Rachel swallowed hard, not knowing what to say.

'Look, Mrs Parker, I don't want to add to your worries, but Anne phoned me last night. We were supposed to go to my aunt's today—'

'Yes,' Rachel nodded. 'I knew.'

'Well, Anne said she wouldn't be going. She seemed upset and I asked if she was all right.'

Miserably he stared at the floor.

'And then what, Graham?'

'Well, to put it bluntly Mrs Parker, Anne said she wasn't going to marry me—just like that. No explanations—nothing!'

Rachel reached out for his hand and held it tightly, not sure if she were giving comfort or seeking it.

'And do you still want to marry Anne—after what has happened today?'

'Of course I do! I love her. But I think she's in need

of help, though.'

'I know she is,' Rachel whispered, 'and the awful part is that I don't know what to do or where to start. I'm her mother, yet I can't get near her. What can I do, Graham?'

She looked into the open, troubled face. She wanted to run her fingers comfortingly through his curly brown hair but she sat still, her whole body rigid with an unknown fear.

'Look, Mrs Parker, it's none of my business, but don't you think you might start at Doctor Lee's?'

'The doctor's?' Rachel's heart gave a little skip. 'Why him? Is Anne ill, Graham? Why didn't I know about it?'

So that was it! Rachel closed her eyes. Why hadn't she realized? Anne was ill or—dear God, no! She couldn't be pregnant?

She sought Graham's eyes and they gazed back into hers, honestly and unwavering.

'What is wrong with Anne? Do you know? Tell me please, Graham?'

'I don't know. I'm not even supposed to know about the times she's been seeing the doctor, either,' he shrugged. 'Anne didn't tell *me*,' he replied, sadly.

'So you think I should try to find out?'

'I don't know. I'm confused as you are. Maybe it won't lead to anything. Doctors won't talk to anybody about a patient—not even to a patient's mother. But the Lees are friends of yours, aren't they? You could try. I'm sure if anyone can help, it will be Doctor Lee. I think you should see him, Mrs Parker. I think you should go—at once!'

* * *

'See Doctor Lee. See him at once!'

Graham Hobson's terse plea had throbbed dully in Rachel's mind for most of the anxious night as she lay wide-eyed, longing for sleep that would not come. By her side, yet a million miles away, John had lain quietly, his breathing deep and even. But nothing ever upset John's nights.

'Problems will still be there in the morning, Rachel,' he always said, 'so why waste sleep in worrying about them?'

That, thought Rachel as she plumped and turned her pillow yet again, was one of the reasons her husband had made it to the top. He was of the rare breed; one who could pigeon-hole his life, place everything into small, distinct compartments with nothing overlapping or interfering. Some time soon, their daughter would have to appear in Court, charged with shop-lifting, but until it happened, John would not let himself be sidetracked. Therefore Anne's troubles would, in the order of things, be slipped into a pigeon-hole in John's mind marked *Marcus James*. Last night John had seen Marcus James and passed the whole matter over to him, for that, according to John's cold logic, was what solicitors were for.

But why, Rachel fretted, haven't we talked about it? Why can't we come together as most families do when trouble comes? But are we a family now, she wondered. And what of Anne? Was she, too, lying awake? Was she yearning for the comfort for which she wouldn't ask—for which she hadn't asked for so long, now. Was it because they had failed her as parents?

Oh Anne, I know how you feel, Rachel yearned, because I too need comfort. I want my husband's arms about me; I want to open my heart to him before it is too late. I need to beg him not to leave for Rotterdam tomorrow, to stay with us and not push us off on to Marcus James.

But John had not stirred in his sleep nor reached out for her in the darkness and as the welcome daylight had filtered through the curtains, Rachel was unashamedly relieved that in a little more than three hours he would be leaving for the airport. Only then would she be free to see their doctor and ask about Anne's visits. Ethically she knew it was all wrong—Graham had reminded her of that last night—but it wouldn't be official; just a Sunday morning back-door visit to her friends, Bill and Joyce Lee. Bill would understand. It couldn't be *that* serious—could it?

'Best not wake Anne up,' John said abruptly as Rachel handed him his second cup of coffee.

'All right,' she whispered, relieved that at least John's departure would be without renewed anger.

'Anyway, that's the car, I think.'

Rachel opened the front door as one of the cars belonging to Parker's Haulage drew up. Beside the driver sat Miss Tremlitt, comfortably unchanging in all the turmoil. She wound down the window and smiled.

'Hullo, Mrs Parker. Are we early?'

They were, as always, exactly on time, Rachel thought, noting the plain brown suit and the travelling coat folded neatly on her lap. Dear Miss T. Safe and anonymous.

'Hullo there,' Rachel smiled back. 'Everything all right at home?'

'Yes, thanks. My sister arrived last night to take over.

It will be a nice change for mother. They'll probably spend the whole time catching up with the Manchester gossip.'

She stopped abruptly as John ran lightly down the steps, responding to his brief nod with an automatic, 'Good morning, Mr Parker.'

Rachel hadn't meant to turn away as John bent to kiss her. She was sorry about it as she watched the car drive slowly away. She seemed always to be sorry these days, she thought dully. Then shaking her shoulders and tilting her chin, she remembered Bill Lee, just a five-minute walk down the tree-lined road, and it made her feel better. Soon now she would start getting to the bottom of things.

Joyce Lee was standing at the cooker when Rachel tapped on the door and walked into the kitchen.

'Hi there, Rachel! You come for coffee or comfort?'

'*Comfort?*'

Rachel stiffened instinctively.

'Hmm. Bill and I saw John at the club last night. Told us he was going away today. Missing him already, uh?'

She grinned teasingly and Rachel relaxed a little. The news hadn't got around—not yet.

'It's Bill I came to see,' she smiled, trying desperately to make her voice sound normal, 'but I'd love a coffee, please.'

'Sure. Himself's in the garden. I'll just set a tray then I'll be with you.'

'Look Joyce—if you don't mind—well, it's a bit awkward...'

She shifted uncomfortably. Joyce Lee was her trusted

friend, but just for the moment Rachel wanted only to talk to Bill.

'Oh, sorry, Rachel. I understand, love. Must say I've thought lately that you've been looking a bit rough,' Joyce smiled. 'Have a word with Bill—he'll soon fix you up. But don't leave without seeing me. I want to talk to you about the wedding.'

She handed the tray to Rachel.

'You'll soon find him. Just follow your nose to that smelly old pipe!'

'Thanks,' Rachel whispered, grateful for her friend's understanding. 'And I *will* tell you about it, Joyce—later.'

Her voice trembled and she tried not to envy Bill and Joyce Lee. Their marriage was so easy-going. They liked each other as well as being deeply and obviously in love. They had three boisterous sons ...

Rachel found Bill in a sheltered corner of the rambling, untidy garden. On the wall behind him a magnolia was bursting into flower. Why, oh why, she yearned, did everything around her have to be so beautiful, so normal, when her own world was somersaulting madly?

'Hullo, Rachel.'

Bill Lee rose to his feet and reached for the tray, his professional eye noting the clenched knuckles, the drawn, pallid face, the blue-black smudges beneath Rachel's eyes.

'Medium, isn't it—no sugar?' he asked without preamble.

'Please.'

'Right, Rachel! What's it all about?'

He passed the cup then smiled gently as her head

shot up and her eyes opened wide with startled intensity.

'Look now, it's me—old Bill—so don't go all uptight. I thought you'd be here, sooner or later. You might even say I've been expecting you!'

Rachel took a gulp of coffee. It burned the back of her throat and made her gasp.

'Then I don't need to tell you I've come about Anne. I know she's been seeing you, Bill.'

'That's right.'

'Well tell me! What's the matter with her? Why didn't I know?'

'She hasn't told you?'

'No. Graham put me on to it last night and he's almost as much in the dark as I am. So what is it?'

'Rachel—Anne's grown up, now,' came the mildly reproving reply. 'I think if she had wanted you to know she'd have told you.'

'Well she didn't, so I'm asking *you*!'

'And you, Rachel Parker, should know better than that. I can't discuss a patient—'

'Look Bill, please don't go all Medical Council on me. I know about ethics and such-like, but this is serious. Anne is in trouble and I think she's sick. I've got to help her. I've got to know!'

'Well, one thing I can tell you, Rachel. Anne isn't pregnant.'

'Oh, thank God,' Rachel breathed, eyes averted, glad that Bill Lee sat unspeaking as she struggled to quieten her emotions.

'I'm sorry I asked you about Anne,' she said, eventually. 'I should have known better—but let me tell you what's happened then maybe you can give *me* some advice. Surely your Hippocratic conscience allows you that much?'

'Yes, Rachel, it very well might, especially since I think you are as much in need of help as Anne is.'

His understanding made Rachel want to weep but she swallowed hard on her tears and said,

'Anne's got into trouble with the police. She was arrested yesterday afternoon for shop-lifting. We got her out on bail ...'

She took another steadying gulp at her coffee, willing herself to go on.

'Anne took a locket—a little heart-shaped thing—worth a few shillings.'

The words came then like a torrent of water when flood-gates have been opened, leaving out nothing from the nightmare at the police station to John's seemingly uncaring attitude.

'He didn't have to go to Holland,' she finished. 'He went to the golf club and saw Marcus James and after that it seemed it just wasn't his problem any more—like when Anne got into trouble at school. He smoothed that over, too—the stealing and the attack on a girl. You didn't know about that, did you Bill?'

'Oh yes, I knew,' he replied, setting a match to his pipe. 'Anne told me and I think I've got that bit worked out. You're her mother, you see. You're too close to the problem.'

'Then tell me what is wrong, please?' Rachel pleaded. 'And don't use any of your big words, Bill.'

'All right. Now, what passed between Anne and myself is private, but what it all boils down to is her natural mother. Anne used the phrase Other Mother when she talked to me, and that's a good sign, Rachel. It told me that in Anne's mind, *you* are her mother, but somewhere in the background is the woman who bore her. Out of loyalty to you, Anne called her the *other* mother. She has a need to know about that other mother, perhaps even to meet her. That's why she came to me. She feels guilty about that need because you have always been so good and loving to her. Do you understand me?'

'Yes Bill, I think I do. I even think I know when she started worrying about her real—her *other*—mother. She knew she was adopted and it never bothered her—not until something happened at school.'

'I'm inclined to agree with you there, Rachel, but I met with a blank wall when I tried to find out what triggered off that particular trouble. Somehow, you'll have to find that out for yourself.'

He smiled encouragement.

'Do you think you can handle it?'

'I don't know.'

She rose to her feet, her whole body numb.

'I really don't know, Bill, but thanks anyway. I'll see you—officially—later on. Maybe I could do with a tonic, or something. And if you like, you can tell Joyce about all this ...'

She placed her empty cup on the tray then walked quickly away. She didn't remember the walk back to Fair Oaks. She only knew she had never felt so alone or apprehensive in the whole of her life.

Anne was sitting at the kitchen table, her dressing-gown thrown loosely around her shoulders, her feet bare, her red-gold hair unbrushed and tied back into a ribbon. She toyed with a half-empty glass of milk and as Rachel came in she looked up and smiled. Gratefully, Rachel smiled back.

'Not you too, Anne?' she said, tracing small circles round her eyes with her forefingers, sad that her daughter's soft young face bore also the unmistakable ravages of an unhappy and sleepless night.

'Sorry, Mum,' she whispered, eyes downcast, 'I seem to be a right little nuisance ...'

'Well, we're over the worst, now.'

It was stilted small-talk, Rachel realized, but at least they had made a start. For all that, though, she knew she would have to step as carefully as if the floor on which she stood was made of egg-shells.

'You been out, Mum?'

'Just for a quick walk—nowhere in particular.'

The lie came easily.

'I suppose Dad's gone?'

'Yes. Up and away with Miss T.'

'Graham's mother phoned.'

'Oh?' Rachel's head jerked up. 'What did she want?'

'You Mum, really, but she managed to hint in passing that didn't I think it might be a good thing if Graham and I were to put the wedding off for a while —like forever; like they didn't want a sneak-thief in the family!'

Her face crumpled and she closed her eyes tightly for a moment, then tossing high her head she said,

'I don't want her precious son, anyway!'

But you do, Anne, Rachel thought, her heart thumping with silent grief. You love each other and need each other and it isn't fair

'Old cat!' Rachel exploded. 'How on earth did she ever manage to have a son as nice as Graham!'

She slammed the percolator on to the hotplate, her jaw clamped tightly, feeling that soon something inside her would explode. And she had been going to stay calm, hadn't she—play it by ear?

'Ugh!' she gasped, then grinning weakly, she picked up a strand of her blue-black hair in a comic gesture.

'Sorry about that outburst. Must be my Latin blood!'

She had intended it to be a joke—to be anything that would help cancel out the implications of Mrs Hobson's hurtful remarks, but Anne's face flushed an angry red and she jumped to her feet, her blue eyes wide and hurt.

'Stop it, Mother! It's all right for you! You can make jokes like that, but I can't, can I?'

'Anne love?' Bewildered, Rachel shook her head. 'What's wrong. I was joking. You know I was.'

'Yes, but it's all right to joke, isn't it, when you've had a father and mother you can remember; when you know that your grandpa married a lady's maid who was Spanish. But what do I know about *my* blood, except that it's *bad*!'

So that was it!

Throwing aside all pretence Rachel grasped Anne roughly by the shoulders.

'*What—do—you—mean?*' she demanded slowly, each quietly emphasized word indicating that this time she wanted, and would have, an answer.

'Tell me Anne,' she insisted. 'What do you mean— *bad blood?*'

'Don't you know? Didn't you realize that people like me have it when their mother's a tart!'

'I'm your mother!' Rachel flung.

'I mean my *real* mother ...'

'*I'm* your real mother!'

'All right then—my other mother—the one who had me. *She* was a tart. She must have been, mustn't she?'

Rachel clenched her fingers into her daughter's shoulders and felt an answering wince of pain. She closed her eyes, desperately forcing back the anger that stormed inside her.

'Listen Anne,' she jerked. 'The girl who had you *wasn't* like that! The tarts you're talking about don't get pregnant! Your other mother could have been someone like you, or me. She didn't go to some back-street abortionist, did she? She had you, Anne, then gave you up for adoption, so you could have a better chance than she could give you, so that some woman like me who was breaking her heart for a child could have you!'

Rachel took a deep, sobbing breath.

'Call your mother what you like, Anne. As far as I'm concerned, I've thanked God every day that she was sensible enough—yes, and brave enough—to part with you, so never, *ever*, call her a tart again!'

She loosed her hands then and let them fall to her sides, physically drained by her outburst. Biting hard on her lips to hold back the sobs that choked in her throat she tried to breathe deeply, but her shoulders were heaving uncontrollably and the pain in her chest made her cry out in anguish.

In that instant Anne's arms were round her and they clung together, each steeped in her own private misery.

'I'm sorry, Mum. I'm so sorry. But can't you try to understand what it's like—wondering who I am and what I am and what's going to come out in my children?'

'Listen! You're *my* Anne, that's who you are,' Rachel

soothed. 'There's nothing that could come out in your children. Where did all this come from? How did you get such silly ideas into your head? Why didn't you ask me?'

'I wanted to, Mum. I really wanted to, but I didn't want to hurt you. I think I was afraid to know the truth, too.'

'But I've told you the truth, Anne. I think your other mother was a nice person. She must have been,' Rachel smiled, blinking away her tears, 'else how could she have had you?'

'And you don't think there's bad blood in me?'

'Bad blood? There isn't such a thing, so it couldn't have been passed on—truly, it couldn't.'

Then suddenly it was all clear to Rachel. It seemed so obvious that she wondered why it had eluded her for so long. Gently she cupped her daughter's face between her hands and said,

'All this started at school, didn't it Anne? That girl you hurt ... ?'

'Yes. You see, I'd got the part of the princess in the school play and I think she was mad about it. But she said she didn't care. She said they'd most likely given it to me because they were sorry for girls like me who had tarts for mothers!'

'So you flew at her?'

'I wanted to *kill* her,' Anne whispered passionately. 'Honest Mum, she made me feel as if I'd crawled out of the gutter. I can't get it out of my mind—even yet; it's awful, not knowing.'

'And the locket? You took that because you wanted help?'

'I don't know—not for sure.' She puckered up her forehead. 'Perhaps in a roundabout way maybe I did. But I remember thinking as I took it, "This is the kind of cheap muck my tart of a mother would give me to wear on my wedding day!"'

'But Dad and I had bought you a Victorian locket pretty much the same.'

'Yes, but the turquoises are real in that one and it's set round with seed pearls. It must have cost quite a bit. The one my other mother would have given me would be cheap and tarty, like her—or like that cat at school said she was.'

She looked pleadingly into Rachel's face.

'Don't you see, Mum, that locket was all my other mother could have afforded. Can you understand? Sometimes, you see, I hated her for my bad blood and other times I wanted to stick up for her. I don't know what to think about her. I used to imagine running away and finding her—not leaving you and Dad—just seeing if I could get to know what she was really like.'

'*... She has a need to learn about that other mother —perhaps even to meet her ...*'

Bill Lee's words came back to Rachel and she knew he had been right. Anne would have to meet that other mother and soon, before the torment inside her became an incurable phobia. Without weighing the wisdom or the folly of what she was about to say, Rachel took a deep breath.

'All right,' she whispered, 'if that's what you truly want, Anne, I'll find her ...'

'You'll what?'

The girl raised a pale, tear-drenched face, her eyes wide with mingled disbelief and wonder.

'*You'll find my other mother?*'

And despite the familiar nagging she felt in the pit of her stomach, despite the voice that screamed,

'Fool! Leave it alone! You don't know what you are starting!' inside her head, Rachel heard herself answering calmly,

'Yes, Anne. No matter what—I'll find her for you—*I promise!*'

THREE

'I'll find her ... I promise.'

It was then that the enormity of Rachel's decision struck her with the impact of a physical blow.

What have I done? she thought wildly. Where will it end? And if I fail, what will be the effect upon Anne?

And what would John say when she told him, Rachel thought, briefly apprehensive. But he would be glad—of course he would—she reasoned.

She felt the pressure of Anne's hand in hers and it gave her courage. She must not be afraid when surely nothing but good could come from such a search.

'Well?' she said breathlessly, lifting her shoulders in a gesture of bewilderment.

It came as a mild shock to realize that suddenly the woman who had borne Anne was no longer a nameless, faceless being. Now she had a name, had assumed an identity; she was the Other Mother.

'That's it, then?'

'That's it, Mum.'

Anne's voice was gentle as she leaned over and kissed Rachel's cheek and in that gesture of reconciliation, Rachel knew that no matter how bleak or frustrating things might become, or how much opposition she might face, she would keep her promise.

They ate their evening meal from trays in the summer-room and talked more companionably together than they had done for a long time.

'You know,' Anne said quietly, 'I'm just beginning to realize how lucky I am—working at Dad's place, I mean. What would have happened, do you suppose, if I'd had to go in to work tomorrow and tell them about everything?'

'Hmm. See what you mean.'

Often in the past, Rachel recalled, she had doubted the wisdom in allowing Anne to work at Parker's Haulage, but now, for the first time, she was glad.

'But the question doesn't arise does it, because you don't need to tell them—not unless you want to.'

'Not just yet,' Anne shook her head, 'but I'm going in tomorrow, as usual. I just couldn't sit around here —wondering.'

Anne was right, Rachel reasoned. It was better that way. There were things to be done, too, that she wanted to do alone; things Anne must not become involved with, yet.

The telephone purred a welcome interruption from the sitting-room.

'Go on then, lazy-bones,' Rachel urged. 'Answer it.'

Most likely it would be Graham, she thought with a surge of hope. He and Anne needed to talk, to sort things out, to make up.

As if she could look into Rachel's mind Anne said, 'You get it, will you Mum? It might be Graham and I don't want to talk to him. Tell him I'm out?'

'But you can't do that. It isn't right!'

'Oh Mum. Why won't you accept it?'

The young face set itself into the all too familiar mask of truculence.

'The wedding's off. There's nothing anybody can do about it!'

Abruptly as it started, the phone stopped ringing and Anne's eyes closed in momentary relief.

'It isn't any use,' she persisted. 'I can't marry Graham —not after this—not when I don't love him any more.'

She shrugged with exaggerated disinterest.

'Anyway, it was most likely Dad, to let you know he's arrived.'

'It wasn't Dad,' Rachel returned, more angrily than she had intended. 'You know he never phones unless it's absolutely necessary.'

She took a deep, steadying breath.

'Listen, love,' she said more gently. 'Graham loves you, I know it. Don't shut him out? Don't ruin both your lives because of what's happened?'

But Anne had risen to her feet.

'I'm going to bed,' she whispered, her face white and strained. 'Don't disturb me if the phone goes again.'

Briefly she brushed Rachel's cheek with her lips.

'Good night, mother.'

Rachel sighed despairingly. For just a little while Anne had relaxed, had even unbended, but now, as always, the old reserve was back again.

Resolutely Rachel lifted her shoulders and tilted her chin. She just had to find Anne's other mother. Things *must* come right for her daughter. She would make them come right, because she knew with absolute certainty that if she did not, not only Anne's happiness was at risk, but that too of herself and John.

As if to make up for last night's outburst, Anne tried to eat the breakfast set before her. Each of them had slept better and arisen a little less tense. Now cautiously, they discussed Rachel's plans.

'I shall start in Manchester,' she said firmly.

'And do you really think you'll have any luck, Mum?'

'I don't see why not. When I explain to the people at the Adoption Society, I'm sure they will understand. And there's the vicar, too. He was very good when we got you—he helped us so much.'

Rachel was glad they had kept in touch with James Whitaker, the vicar from their Manchester-time. They still exchanged Christmas cards and every year, on Anne's birthday, John gave Rachel a cheque to send to the restoration fund at the old church where Anne had been christened. Mr Whitaker would help her, of that at least Rachel was quietly optimistic.

The crunching of wheels on the gravel driveway broke into her thoughts.

'Now who's that?' she demanded as the door-chimes jangled.

'Maybe the post van with a parcel,' Anne scraped back her chair. 'I'll get it.'

Rachel smiled. Perhaps it was Graham?

'Oh!'

She heard Anne's voice, slightly surprised, then a whispered,

'Good morning.'

'Are you Anne Vanessa Parker?'

Head tilted, Rachel smelled fear. The strange voice was too formal and it sent a shiver to the tips of her fingers.

Quickly she made for the hall. At the open door stood a uniformed policeman. He was young with a face that ironically was strangely like Graham's.

Transfixed, Rachel saw Anne's nod of reply as she took the buff envelope that was held towards her.

'Thank you, miss. Good morning.'

It took only a few seconds.

Still unable to move, Rachel heard the ripping of the envelope then Anne turned, her eyes wide with fear, a piece of pale blue paper in her hand. She ran her tongue round her lips then said in a strange, desperate voice,

'It's the summons. I've got to go to Court—on Thursday...'

'*Thursday?* But that's barely three days!'

'I know,' Anne whispered. 'Maybe it's because I pleaded guilty—'

Suddenly the fearsome paralysis loosed its hold on Rachel. Looking at her watch she said,

'I'll give it half an hour then I'll phone Marcus James.' Panic was churning inside her. Desperately she hoped it didn't show. 'Meantime, there's nothing either of us can do. Best you should go to work as normal, love—keep your mind off things, uh?'

'Are you going to let Dad know?'

Anne's voice trembled with apprehension.

'If Mr James thinks I should. He'll know best,' Rachel comforted briskly. 'If he thinks Dad should come back, then he'll soon be in touch with him.'

'Oh Mum. What will I do?' Anne pleaded.

Rachel bent down to pick up the envelope then took the summons and folded it away. Placing her arm round the dejected young shoulders she said,

'You'll go upstairs and get dressed and when you feel up to it you can take the Mini and drive yourself in to work.'

She wanted to take her daughter and hold her tightly,

kiss away her fears as she had been able to do when Anne was a little girl. But those days were long gone, Rachel thought sadly.

'Come on then,' she said with a brightness she did not feel. 'Let's not worry any more than we need, uh? It'll be all right—you'll see!'

'Yes,' Anne repeated tonelessly. 'Let's not worry.'

Oh, John, Rachel yearned as she watched the sad little figure slowly climbing the stairs. If only you knew how much we need you, Anne and me. But John was in Rotterdam and he didn't know she was afraid; afraid for Anne, for herself, for everything.

She bit on her lip until it hurt. She was lonely and she needed a shoulder to cry on. But she wouldn't cry —not until tomorrow. Tomorrow was the best time for useless, too-late tears. Tilting her chin still higher, Rachel placed the buff envelope by the telephone. As soon as Anne had left for work, she decided, she would ring Marcus James's office and after that, she thought bitterly, nothing would ever be quite the same again.

Rachel closed the book she was trying to read. This time tomorrow, she thought, it will be all over. She was grateful for the calm assurance of their solicitor. John had been right, Rachel was forced to admit.

'Leave it to Marcus James,' he had said. 'He's the expert.'

But it was different for men, she reasoned. Men thought with their heads, never with their hearts.

The telephone rang and John's voice was so clear that he could have been calling from Parker's depot.

'Are you all right?' he demanded without preamble. 'Sorry I didn't phone before this. I've been out of town for a couple of days, visiting contacts—just got the message Marcus left. What is it?'

'John! Anne's in court tomorrow!'

'*Tomorrow?* But that's ridiculous! I'd have thought it would be ages before—'

'Listen—*please?* I think it will be all right. Marcus is very hopeful. And he's got Bill Lee to speak for Anne.'

'What on earth can Bill do? What's it got to do with him?' John demanded impatiently. 'What do they need a medico's evidence for?'

'Oh, it's a long story, but I think I've found what's been bothering Anne. She told Bill about it. Bill wouldn't give me much to go on, but it's all tied up with her need to know her natural mother. I think Bill is right and I want to help Anne to find her.'

'But you *can't* believe all that nonsense!' John cajoled. 'It's a lot of old rubbish and I don't like the idea of it at all. Anne's our daughter, Rachel—she's our chosen daughter—and that's all she needs to know. Bill Lee's an old woman! Don't let him put ideas into your head —all right?'

Rachel wanted to argue, to reason, to plead even, but she bit back her words. Bill Lee wasn't wrong. Anne's need to know her other mother was very real and she, Rachel, had promised to help. She took a deep breath then said,

'All right, John. If that's how you feel...'

It was useless, she reasoned silently. Men like John just didn't understand.

'Of course that's how I feel! It's not a good idea at all. Forget it, Rachel—all right?'

Rachel sighed into the phone.

'All right,' she replied, tonelessly.

There was a small pause between them, a few embarrassed seconds that stretched into an eternity before John said,

'Look, Rachel, I'll cut off now and get hold of Marcus. If he thinks I should come back, I'll get the next plane out. Miss T. can see to things, here ...'

Wearily Rachel shook her head.

'You can't, John. We're in Court at ten o'clock. You'd never make it. We'll manage—really we will.'

'You're sure now? You'll be all right?'

'Yes John.'

'And Anne? Give her my love. Look, I *will* get back if you want me to, Rachel.'

It was then she should have said,

'*Yes, please come, John. Anne needs you and I need you too. I want you to hold me and tell me it will all come right, like you used to do ...*'

But the words remained unspoken and she said, instead,

'No, don't do that. You were right. Marcus James knows what he's doing. We'll be fine, truly we will.'

A sickness washed over her as she laid down the receiver. She felt like a woman cut into two pieces. The wife in her ached for the comfort of her man but the mother-part knew she wanted John to stay in Rotterdam. No matter how much John pooh-poohed the idea she would keep her promise to Anne. Best that John should be away for a while; best that he didn't come home yet, to stop her.

Rachel leaned back her head and closed her eyes, willing herself to be calm, whilst a mixture of fear and excitement churned inside her.

The train rocked on, just half an hour away from Manchester. Could it really be less than a week ago that the telephone call had summoned them to the police station in Birmingham? Was it only yesterday that the Magistrate had said, sternly and without compromise,

'The fact that you did not need steal in no way diminishes the seriousness of what you have done, but in view of your doctor's assurance that you were under stress at the time of the offence, the Bench has decided to deal leniently with you on this occasion.'

There had followed then a demand that Anne should be of good behaviour and the warning that another appearance in Court would be treated with the utmost gravity. And all the while Anne stood there, white-faced and alone as a fine of twenty-five pounds and costs were awarded against her.

'I don't know what to say,' Rachel gasped. 'I just can't thank you both enough.' Gratefully she addressed Marcus James and Bill Lee as together they left the Magistrates' Court.

'All in a day's work,' their solicitor replied cheerfully as he left them to hurry away to another Court and another case. But Bill Lee took Rachel aside.

'This is just the beginning—you realize that, don't you?' he asked quietly.

'Yes, and I know what's to be done, Bill. Trouble is that John isn't keen on the idea at all.'

'Well, that's for the two of you to decide and I can't interfere,' he replied, 'but remember, I gave you my opinion when you came to see me, Rachel, and nothing has happened since then to make me change my mind. Still,' he smiled, 'you'll work something out between you, I hope, if only for Anne's sake.'

'Don't worry, we will,' Rachel assured him as they walked towards the car park. Or at least *she* would she thought grimly, raising her hand to wave him good-bye. What was more, she realized as panic arose afresh inside her, she had very little time in which to do it. She knew John was against what she was going to do and she hated deceiving him. There had never been secrets between them, but she'd got to keep her promise to Anne, Rachel asserted silently, even at the risk of trouble between John and herself.

She spun round as she heard her name called and felt pleasure at the sight of Graham Hobson's face.

'I've been in Court—I hope you didn't mind. I tried to catch Anne's eye but I don't think she saw me. Would it be all right, Mrs Parker, if I had just a few words alone with her before you leave?'

'But of course, Graham. Come to think of it, why don't you drive Anne back to Fair Oaks then stay and have a cup of tea with us?' Rachel retorted, unashamedly interfering.

'Thanks,' Graham laughed. 'I'll drive slowly—the long way home!'

But Anne, who waited silently by Rachel's car would have none of it.

'Can't you leave me alone?' she flung. 'Don't you think I've had enough for one day? Why won't you accept it, Graham? *I'm not going to marry you!*'

Rachel stood helplessly by, not knowing whether to take Anne and shake sense into her stubborn head or comfort Graham whose eyes were filled with hurt and bewilderment.

'Anne!' she jerked. 'How can you be so cruel, so utterly stupid?'

'Oh, it comes easily to someone like me whose mother was no better than she need have been!'

'Look! Say that just once more Anne, and—'

Rachel stopped, aware that their voices were loud and angry and that a public car-park was no place for a show-down with her daughter. She turned beseechingly to Graham.

'I think maybe I'd better go, but don't think I shall give up, Anne,' Graham said quietly as he walked away. 'I still want to marry you. Nothing will change that.'

Rachel flung her hat and handbag on to the back seat of the car. She was angry and saddened that Anne should seem set upon ruining both her own life and Graham's. She drove tight-lipped until the city-centre was behind them and they were heading for open country.

'I think you behaved abominably, Anne. I'm ashamed of you,' she choked, unable any longer to hold her feelings in check. 'If I were Graham, I wouldn't give you a second thought!'

'That's roughly the idea,' Anne replied, stony-faced. 'And even if I loved him, how do you think I could live with his mother's constant disapproval?'

'You're not marrying his mother!'

'Don't? *Please?* I'm not marrying him, Mum. I'm not marrying anybody!'

'I see,' Rachel replied, flatly. 'Then there doesn't seem anything more to say, does there?'

'Oh Mum—I'm sorry, truly I am. You've been just marvellous over all this and I don't know how to thank you enough. But I've been sick with worry about it and all I want to do just now is to try to forget it. I shouldn't have flared up like I did, but I couldn't help it.'

'All right,' Rachel had retorted more gently. 'I understand. I think we're both a bit edgy ...'

The braking of the train jerked Rachel's thoughts away from the unhappiness of the previous day. They were pulling into Manchester now. In just a few minutes, she realized, she would be standing at James Whitaker's door.

Heart beating, she pulled on her gloves. There was no going back, now.

The taxi in which Rachel sat halted yet again and she took a deep breath and tried to relax. There was plenty of time, she told herself. She wasn't due at the vicarage until 11.30. She hadn't told James Whitaker what she wanted to see him about. If she were honest, she had leaned over backwards not to.

'I shall be in Manchester tomorrow,' she said, over the phone. 'Could I call in and see you?'

He had been delighted and Rachel felt a stab of guilt. She was still feeling guilty when John phoned from his Rotterdam hotel later that same evening.

'How did it go, Rachel? How was it?'

He had been pleased and relieved when she told him everything was just fine—that Anne hadn't even been placed on probation.

'What will you do, now?'

'Oh, I don't know, John. Try to unwind, I suppose; catch up with the housework—let down the hem of my red skirt,' she lied.

'Well, don't do anything silly—we'll talk about Anne when I get back—all right?'

'Okay.'

She knew what John meant. She was being warned-off, she knew it. No looking for Anne's other mother...

'I'll probably go into town and get my hair done,' she said, warming to her deceit, hating herself for it, knowing that even as she had spoken she was already committed to going to Manchester.

Rachel sighed and looked around her. It was more than eighteen years since she was last here, she realized with surprise. They had come up from Birmingham for the signing of Anne's adoption papers. Mr Whitaker was in the Children's Court that day and the lady from the Adoption Society. It had all gone through very smoothly, she recalled. She wondered afterwards why she had worried so.

Eighteen years, she mused. So much had happened since then; so very much.

James Whitaker had changed very little with the passing of time. His round, pink face was a little more lined, his hair a little whiter, but the smile was the same—warm and welcoming. He was pleased to see Rachel, glad to be able to thank her personally for their generosity to his church over the years, eager for news of Anne and John.

'Why, she must be grown up by now, Mrs Parker?'

'Indeed she is—and soon to be married.'

Mentally Rachel crossed her fingers.

'In fact, vicar, that's really why I'm here.'

She hesitated for a moment then said,

'It's a bit difficult and maybe a bit unethical—'

She stopped, embarrassed, but his smile gave her the encouragement she needed and taking a deep breath she told him her story, grateful that he made no attempt to interrupt her.

'So you see, Mr Whitaker, it's very important to Anne, and to me, too, that we find her other mother,' Rachel finished, breathlessly. 'I am certain she was a decent girl and it seems wrong that the happiness of two young people should be put at risk just because of a schoolgirl's malice.'

She paused, amazed at her eloquence then said softly, 'You do understand, don't you? You *will* help?'

James Whitaker placed his fingertips together and regarded them gravely.

'What does your husband have to say about all this, Mrs Parker?'

Rachel's head shot up.

'What I mean to say, my dear, is have you talked to him about it?'

'Well—he's not exactly in favour of it,' Rachel prevaricated. 'In fact, I think he's against it, but he will come to see my point of view, Mr Whitaker, I know he will.'

The elderly man rose abruptly to his feet.

'Can I make you a coffee?' he said, picking his way across the crowded little study, switching on a kettle that stood on the broad window ledge amid a clutter of books and collecting-boxes.

Rachel nodded, wishing she could see his face. He was standing with his back to her, spooning instant coffee into gaudy yellow mugs and he seemed to be hesitating, searching for words. After a while he said,

'It might be a little difficult, Mrs Parker. You see, the adoption people don't like giving out such information and I'm afraid I can't help you much, either. I'm semi-retired these days and I don't do as much as I used to. I'm not connected with the Mother and Baby Home or the Adoption Society at all now. The Government took it over some years ago and I must confess it was a relief to me. It was hard, sometimes, finding the money to keep it going.'

He turned to face her, more composed, now. Rachel Parker was a good woman, he thought, and he wanted to let her down lightly. He didn't want to be too hurtful, too brusque.

'We found homes for a great many babies,' he said gently, 'but I was only one of a committee of ten. My memory isn't so good, nowadays. Why don't you go to the Home and tell them what you have just told me, my dear? If there is a way of helping you, I am sure that Matron will know of it.'

He sighed inwardly, his conscience nagging him painfully. He was passing the buck, he admitted it, and to one who could demolish Rachel's quest in a few short, efficient sentences. It wasn't possible, he argued silently, even for the best of reasons, to give Rachel Parker the information she wanted. He felt like Judas as, secure in the knowledge that her search would soon come to an abrupt end, he offered her a digestive biscuit.

'That's it. Go and see Matron and be sure to tell me how you get on, Mrs Parker. I shall be most interested to know.'

He sighed and spooned sugar into his coffee. Really, he thought sadly, being a parish priest could be very trying at times, very trying indeed.

As she paid-off the taxi outside the Home in which Anne had been born, Rachel was unprepared for the changes that had taken place. The drab green woodwork of the windows had been replaced by shining white and the front door painted a bright golden-yellow. Spring flowers bloomed where once gloomy, soot-stained bushes stood. Memories rushed in as Rachel recalled that day on which the gentle-voiced Scottish matron placed Anne in her arms, gently crooning,

'There now, wee one. Away with your mother and father, now.'

Blue eyes had gazed upwards and tiny, perfect fingers stretched themselves around Rachel's. The little face had been so innocent, so vulnerable and trusting, she remembered. She had driven home with a trembling smile on her lips and tears of pure joy on her cheeks.

'She's all yours,' Matron said. 'Her mother called her Anne...'

The yellow door was opened by a young, slim woman. She wore a white overall, tight-belted into a slight waist. Her hair was short cut and fair and she wore no cap.

'Good morning. Mrs Parker, isn't it? How thoughtful of you to ring first.'

'You're the Matron?' Rachel gasped. And she couldn't have been a day over thirty! Not like the one Rachel remembered—middle-aged and comfortably plump.

'I can only give you a few minutes, I'm afraid. Shall we talk in my office?'

Bemused, Rachel sat cautiously on the edge of her chair, waiting in vain for the efficient young woman to introduce herself but she said instead,

'How can I help you?'

'I want to know where I can find my adopted daughter's mother,' Rachel rushed in blindly. 'I know such a request isn't usual, but believe me it is very important.'

'It is not at all unusual, Mrs Parker,' came the terse interruption, 'although I must admit it is rarely the adoptive mother who makes the request.'

'You mean, people have asked you before?'

'Frequently. What is more, we always give the same answer and that is "*Sorry*".'

'You mean you won't help me? But if you would listen—let me explain—I know you would want to. Believe me, I don't ask lightly.'

'I'm quite sure you don't, Mrs Parker, but nevertheless, I cannot help. I am not allowed to.'

The younger woman stood up, indicating firmly that the interview was over.

'I know it must sound extremely heartless, Mrs Parker, but what do you imagine would happen if I were to tell every young girl who asked me, where she could find her natural mother, or if I were to tell every woman who has signed away her baby the whereabouts of that child?'

She shrugged eloquently.

'There would be chaos, wouldn't there and heart-break, too? You say you want to find your daughter's natural mother? But does that woman want to be found? Please take my advice,' she said as she held open the door. 'However good your reasons, let this thing drop —forget it. Sooner or later you are going to have to, you know.'

Forget it!

The words were still pounding inside Rachel's head as she boarded the Birmingham train. She had been so sure that in Manchester she would at least have been given some help, some hope, but instead she had met only with embarrassed prevarication on the one hand and a polite but firm refusal on the other.

It might have been different if the old Matron had been there, Rachel pondered. She would have helped. Where was she now, that cheerful little body? Dismayed, Rachel realized that she couldn't even recall her name.

It'll come, she thought. It's on the tip of my tongue. Mac—? Mac-what-was-it? Tantalizingly, the name eluded her.

Dejectedly she slumped into a corner seat. She had achieved nothing except to waste a precious day. What had John said? *Anne is our chosen daughter. Leave it.*

And now what would she tell Anne, Rachel thought with sudden alarm. She had been so confident, hadn't she? How, having raised Anne's hopes, could she admit that so far she had drawn a blank?

But she didn't have to tell Anne—not tonight. Thankfully Rachel remembered that at least her daughter would not be at Fair Oaks when she got back.

'I want to go away for a few days,' Anne had said. 'I half promised Maggie I'd go to her place, if things turned out all right at the Court.'

Motherless Maggie Dean—the only real friend Anne had ever made, who lived with her father in an old Victorian semi on the other side of town. Maggie, who was to have been Anne's bridesmaid.

'I shall still go in to work, Mum. It's just that I want to get out of Graham's way for a bit—think about things—sort myself out.'

Rachel had offered no resistance. A week in Maggie's sensible company could do nothing but good, she reasoned and with Anne away she would be better able to get on with the job of finding the other mother. And that way too, Anne would not become too involved—not until she had to. Rachel was glad that tonight, at least, she wouldn't have to tell Anne of her failure.

'What will I do?' she demanded silently of her reflection in the train window. 'Where do I go from here?'

FOUR

Rachel was still asking herself that question as she left the train and joined the small queue at the taxi-rank outside the station. Digging her hands into her pockets to wait she looked with disinterest at a hoarding that invited her to Keep Britain Tidy, to Spend a Mini-Weekend in London, to ...

She screwed up her eyes. The advertisement was so small she could hardly read it from where she stood.

Daniel Steele. Inquiry Agent. 24-hour service.

The address and telephone number were printed below.

An Inquiry Agent? She'd never have thought of it. Hope surged through her afresh. Why not? What had she to lose? And honestly, did she have any choice? On an impulse she read the address again, then committing it to memory, walked resolutely to find it.

At the bend in the linoleum-covered stairs a notice pointed upwards to Daniel Steele's office. Above the door, a lighted fanlight indicated that he was still working, Rachel realized with relief. If the office had been closed it would have been the last straw and she would have sat down on those shabby stairs and wept, she vowed. A piece of paper pinned to the door requested that she should knock and enter.

Inside, an unshaded light-bulb accentuated the bare-ness of the place. A worn carpet covered most of the floor but the windows were uncurtained. In the corner stood a wash-basin and by it a small table which held a kettle, cups and a couple of tins. Filing cabinets stood against one wall and in the centre of the room, directly below the glaring light, a man sat at a large desk, his face flushing an angry red as he almost snapped into the telephone,

'Then I'm sorry, Mr Collins, but you'll find as you go along that gathering evidence for divorce proceedings is *not* a pleasant task! Good night to you!'

The man with the lined face laid down the phone then looked up, allowing a smile that was just enough to move his lips. Reaching out for the jacket that hung on his chair he rose to his feet.

'Dan Steele,' he said, indicating a chair. 'What can I do for you?'

His approach was direct and it caught Rachel off guard.

'Do you find missing persons, Mr Steele?' she asked, eventually.

'Yes.' The reply was tinged with caution. 'Who is it? A son ... a daughter?'

'No, nothing like that. Maybe I'm misleading you,' Rachel hazarded. 'Have you time to listen to me tonight? I'll be as brief as I can.'

Steele nodded, unspeaking, and for the first time since she had come into the room, Rachel looked properly at him.

A button was missing from his shirt and his thick hair was in need of a trim. He looked—she had to search for the word—neglected? But that didn't make him any the less a good Inquiry Agent, she hastened.

And he was tall and broad-shouldered and looked well able to take care of himself, should the need arise. She thought, in fact, that if she were in a tight corner, it might well be someone like Daniel Steele she would choose to be alongside her.

She blushed, aware that he was returning her gaze with equal frankness and without so much the flickering of an eyelid.

'I'm sorry,' Rachel said, dropping her eyes at once, 'only it'll be the third time I've told this story today. I just hope *you'll* listen to me.'

'Lady, for ten pounds a day and expenses, I listen to most things, provided they're within the limits of the law!'

His brusqueness pulled Rachel up with a jerk and she said tightly,

'The woman I want to find isn't missing in the accepted sense of the word. I don't know her name or even what she looks like. I only know I've got to find her.'

'That's a pretty tall order.'

'I know.'

Tired now and utterly dejected, Rachel told him what she had told James Whitaker and what she had tried to tell the brisk young matron at the Home.

'... so it's important that I find her, you see,' she finished. 'For my daughter's sake I've got to—'

'Hey there! Hold on a minute!'

His face set with disbelief, Daniel Steele broke into Rachel's explanation.

'You mean to say you want to find your adopted daughter's *real* mother?'

'I do, Mr Steele and I would be grateful for all the help and advice you can give me.'

'Then I'll give it—free! My advice to you is to go home, and forget it!'

'Oh, no! Not you, too! I was so ... so ... sure—'

Blindly she groped in her handbag, tears spilling from her eyes.

'I'm sorry,' she sniffed. 'I can't find my hankie.'

'Here. Be my guest.'

Daniel Steele opened a drawer and took out a box of tissues.

Noisily Rachel blew her nose and dabbed at her eyes then drawing a shuddering breath she looked up and said,

'Forgive me, please. I shouldn't have done that,' she shrugged, 'only no one—just *no one*—seems to want to know.'

The rugged face creased into a grin of amazement. 'You mean it?' he asked. 'You really mean it?'

Rachel looked down at the tightly clenched fingers in her lap and nodded.

There was the briefest of pauses then Steele picked up a pencil and flicked open the pad on his desk.

'All right,' he nodded. His voice was resigned but his eyes were kinder, now. 'Just give me your name and address, then begin at the beginning ...'

Rachel left out nothing. She was grateful to Daniel Steele for agreeing to listen to her and for that reason was determined to be scrupulously honest, not only with him but with herself, too.

When she had finished speaking, she sat with her hands clenched tightly in her lap, staring fixedly at the floor. There was no sound in the room save the ticking of an unseen clock and the ponderous tapping of Steele's pencil against his teeth.

'What was the Matron's name?' he said, suddenly. 'The old one—the one you liked.'

'It was Mac—'

Rachel shook her head.

'Oh, I don't know,' she said, desperately. 'All the way back I tried to remember it. I went over conversations we had had together, thinking it might come to me, but it didn't. Anyway, we mostly called her Matron,' she ended, lamely.

'All right—don't worry. The Vicar'll tell us. He asked you to let him know how you got on at the Home, didn't he? Well, give him a ring and tell him, then casually mention the old Matron. It's my bet he'll drop her name without noticing.'

'Don't you think that's being a bit underhanded?'

'Yes, as a matter of fact, I do,' Steele affirmed blandly, 'but I reckon we don't have much choice.'

Without any more prompting Rachel took out her diary and found James Whitaker's number. *We*, Daniel Steele had said. She wasn't on her own any more. She had an ally!

'Okay,' he said, laconically, nodding towards the phone. 'Have a go...'

When she told the Reverend Whitaker of her lack of success at the Mother and Baby Home, Rachel could not be sure whether his reply was laced with sympathy or relief.

'... so I was wondering,' she ended, 'if perhaps the old Matron might be able to help me.'

'Ah, there again I'm afraid I must disappoint you, Mrs Parker. Miss McIver retired ten years ago, and that's a long time, my dear. It would surprise me, even if you were to find her, if she could remember any more than I can.'

'But don't you know where she went, Mr Whitaker? Could she perhaps have gone home to Scotland to retire?'

'I'm afraid I don't know...'

Rachel sighed inwardly but continued doggedly,

'Well, do you think Miss McIver might have left a forwarding address?'

'Oh, I very much doubt that.'

The reply came too readily.

'So. The name was McIver?' Steele said when Rachel put down the phone.

'Yes, but that was all he let slip. He was so vague it just wasn't true. He was stalling, I'll swear he was.'

Steele shrugged.

'Likely he was only trying to save your daughter—and maybe you, Mrs Parker—a load of misery. Vicars don't usually make good liars, anyway,' he added, quirking his mouth downwards, offering his cigarette packet to Rachel.

'Well, we've got ourselves a start. I just might be able to trace your Miss McIver. If she's retired there'll be records somewhere and maybe I could poke about a bit at the Home in Manchester. Leave it with me, uh?' he said, 'and I'll be in touch.'

Reluctantly Rachel rose to her feet.

'I'm very grateful to you, Mr Steele. I hope I haven't kept you too long?'

She looked at her watch, flushing guiltily. She hadn't realized it was nearly nine o'clock.

'That's all right.' Steele's sharp reply was brusque as

he opened the door for her. 'My time's my own, Mrs Parker.'

Fair Oakes seemed strangely empty as Rachel closed the front door behind her. As a matter of habit she walked through the house, snapping on lights and checking that everything was in order.

Anne's room was just as it had been left that morning. Automatically Rachel picked up discarded underwear and a sweater, placing them in the clothes basket. She was both glad and relieved that Anne had decided to stay with Maggie Dean for a few nights; glad because Maggie's company would be good for Anne in her present state of mind; relieved that tonight at least, she would not have to admit to her daughter that so far she had got nowhere and that the success or failure of her search seemed now to depend on the faint hope of finding Miss McIver and the goodwill of an enigmatic Inquiry Agent.

Ponderously Rachel filled the kettle then spooned tea into a pot. Daniel Steele. What a strange man he was—a contradiction of all she had ever imagined an Inquiry Agent to be. He had looked tired—weary almost—and if the state of his ash-tray was anything to go by, had probably existed all day on nothing more than coffee and cigarettes. His jacket was long overdue at the cleaners, Rachel's practical mind decided and his hair was in need of cutting. To have called his office spartan or even functional would have been a kindness. The room in which he worked was downright shabby and if it advertised its occupant's prosperity, then Daniel Steele was well down on his luck. If she had had any sense at all, she would have taken the advice he gave at the onset Rachel thought grimly.

'Go home, Mrs Parker and forget it!'

Yet it was precisely those words that made Rachel want to persist, she realized. They were spoken with honesty and firmness and his eyes, when she looked into them had been disbelieving but kind. She hadn't meant to make a fool of herself, to burst into tears like a spoiled adolescent, but she had been tired, hadn't she, and despondent?

Absently she reached for the biscuit tin. A quick drink, then straight to bed, she thought. And she would allow herself a sleeping-tablet, tonight. No sense in lying awake half the night, worrying. And in the morning she thought with a brief uplifting of hope, there would be someone who might be able to help her—Daniel Steele, Inquiry Agent, who needed a button sewing on his shirt. Strange, she mused as she poured tea into her cup, how that missing button seemed to bother her.

The phone rang at exactly 10.15 the next morning, which wasn't before time, Rachel thought, considering she had been willing it out of its maddening inertia since the moment she got out of bed.

'Steele here, Mrs Parker. I think I've found your Miss McIver.'

'You haven't.' She didn't even try to hide her excitement. 'Oh, so soon! How on earth did you do it?'

'Steady on there,' he retorted, 'I said I *thought* I'd found her. I could be wrong, but I reckon it's worth a quick visit. You game, Mrs Parker? Want to come along?'

'Yes, oh, yes. Where is she living?'

'It's a little place called Lossley, out of Manchester,

going towards Crewe. Would you like to talk to her yourself? We could be there pretty quickly on the motorway. I'll tell you all about it as we go,' he added, not waiting for her reply. 'What say I pick you up in half an hour?'

Rachel rummaged through her wardrobe, wondering whether tweeds and cashmere or a trouser suit would make the most favourable impression on Miss McIver. Discarding both, she settled for a skirt and jerkin with a toning silk blouse.

Daniel Steele had sounded quite pleased with himself, she thought—almost eager to go to Lossley—his near-cynical attitude forgotten. And she was glad she had sought his help. She had tried going it alone and got nowhere. There was something about Steele, she pondered, that gave her confidence—even if he did neglect himself shamefully and sometimes spoke abruptly. And shabby office or not, he *had* found Miss McIver.

Her heart was light as she laid her coat over the hall chair and set her handbag and gloves at the ready beside it, excitement churning inside her. She looked at her watch. In less than ten minutes they would be on their way to a place called Lossley where Miss McIver lived. Daniel Steele was going to be lucky for her, Rachel decided for she felt instinctively that Miss McIver would help her.

Clucking impatiently, she looked at her watch again.

Steele had barely settled Rachel in his car before she asked,

'How did you manage it—and so quickly?'

He shrugged, negotiating a sharp right-turn as he said,

'Luck, I suppose and a bit of the old-pals act. I used to

be in the C.I.D. you see, and once a copper, always a copper. Sometimes I can do them a favour; sometimes they do me one...'

'And?'

'It was a long-shot, I suppose. An old mate of mine let me go through the telephone directories at the local station last night. I banked on finding her in the Manchester book. I'd a feeling, somehow, that she had retired locally, and she had. The fourth phone-call paid off. I think we've got the right one.'

'But you're not sure?'

'As sure as I can be. I had to go carefully on the phone, though. Didn't want to arouse suspicion and make the old lady clam up on me.'

Rachel gave a little smile of pleasure then said, seriously,

'What would have happened if Miss McIver had retired to Glasgow, or Edinburgh? She'd have taken a bit of finding, then.'

'Don't think about it,' Steele quirked down his lips into the bare outline of a smile. 'You'd have had to put your diamonds in hock!'

So Steele thought she was rich, Rachel pondered. He had seen Fair Oaks and probably already connected her with Parker's Haulage—a fact she had been careful to keep to herself. She said, hesitantly,

'Mr Steele, I don't have any diamonds and I haven't a lot of money—not of my own. I shall be able to pay your fees—just about—but that's all.'

He would have thought it strange, she thought, that even though her husband was a wealthy man, the most money she could produce was exactly £250. It had been painstakingly saved from her housekeeping money and the amounts John gave her from time to time for hair-do's or to spend on a lunch in town. John paid all the bills, and she had never needed to ask for money of her own.

Briefly Steele turned in his seat to face her.

'You'll get a fully detailed account, Mrs Parker,' he said curtly, abysmally misinterpreting Rachel's explanation.

'I'm sorry,' she stammered. 'I didn't mean—'

But he was negotiating the motorway slip-road and it was useless, Rachel knew, to say more. But did he have to be quite so touchy?

Steele took the car into the fast lane and settled down to a steady sixty-five, accelerating only when it was necessary to overtake. He drove as well as John, Rachel conceded and she felt safe beside him.

'Do you drive, Mrs Parker?' Steele asked, eventually.

'Yes. I've got a Mini of my own,' she replied, glad to break the silence between them, 'but Anne is using it at present. She's staying with a friend for a few days. She drives very well,' she added, proudly. 'Passed her test the first time. Maybe she gets it from her father.'

'Hmm. He's Parker Haulage, isn't he?'

Rachel nodded, unspeaking.

'And from what you inferred, he doesn't much approve of what you are doing, either.'

'No, he doesn't,' Rachel answered flatly. 'But he's away, you see, and when he comes back, when I've had the chance to talk properly to him, I know he'll agree that I'm doing the right thing.'

'So how long before he's back? How long have we got?'

'A week.' Rachel's reply was apprehensive. 'Do you think we'll have found something by then?'

Steele stared ahead of him, reading the exit sign, flashing left and edging into the slow lane.

'With luck we should have,' he said, his eyes steady on the traffic. 'One way or another ...'

As if to prevent any more questions, he handed Rachel a folded road-map.

'Let's see how good a navigator you are,' he said, 'and it's Lossley we want, remember, not Land's End.'

'Ha!' Rachel retorted, tossing her head, but she smiled as she said it.

They arrived in Lossley a little after midday. It was a tiny place, not much more than a huddle of houses round a tree-bordered green with a stone church at one end and a public house at the other.

All around them, hawthorn hedges were breaking into leaf and a gentle breeze scattered blossom on the Spring grass.

Steele took out his notebook.

'She lives at "Burnside",' he said, winding down the car window and nodding towards a little bridge. 'The cottage by the stream is the one, I shouldn't wonder.'

His stomach felt painfully empty. His breakfast had consisted of a mug of near-cold tea and now he found himself wondering if the landlord at the inn was enlightened enough to provide bar-snacks. Thoughts of bread, cheese, pickles and a glass of beer became almost too much to bear.

The name 'McIver' was plain to see on a small brass plate as they neared the white-painted gate.

'Can I speak to her alone?' Rachel asked. 'I think it

might be best.'

'Sure,' Steele replied, prompted by his stomach. 'I'll take the car and wait for you down the road.' He nodded towards the inn. 'You'll be all right?'

'Yes,' Rachel nodded, crossing her fingers, breathing deeply to steady the thumping in her throat.

'Good luck, then,' Steele said. 'Don't rush it, eh?'

Rachel swallowed hard then lifted the gate-latch. This time, she insisted silently, she was going to be lucky—she just *had* to be!

It seemed an age before the door was opened to her knock.

'Miss McIver?'

'Yes?'

'Oh, no!'

The disappointment in Rachel's voice could not be disguised. This wasn't Matron. The woman in the tweed skirt and hand-knitted sweater was not the woman who had placed Anne in her arms all those years ago.

'I'm sorry, but I think I must have come to the wrong house...'

Tears of frustration sprang to Rachel's eyes and trembled in her voice.

'I was looking for Matron from—'

'Aye. That'll be Nessie, my sister. You'll be wanting her, maybe? Come away in. Who shall I say it is?'

'Rachel Parker.'

The reply was scarcely audible as relief took over. 'I live near Birmingham now, but Miss McIver might remember me. She was matron of the Mother and Baby Home in Manchester—'

'And you were one of her mothers?'

'One of her adoptive mothers,' Rachel smiled, 'and

I'd be so very grateful if she could spare me a few minutes.'

The smell of cooking drifted into the hallway.

'Oh dear. I've not come at an inconvenient time?'

'No, no,' beamed the younger Miss McIver. 'We have our meal prompt at one o'clock, so that'll give you time for a good old blether,' she smiled, nodding towards a half-open door. 'Away in, now. She'll be glad to see you.'

There was no mistaking the elderly lady who sat by the window, her crochet needle painstakingly prodding a white, shawl-like garment.

'Hullo, Matron. Do you remember me—Rachel Parker? It's a long time ago, but you were at the Manchester Home when we adopted our daughter.'

Miss McIver smiled and laid down her work.

'You'll forgive me if I don't get up, Mrs Parker,' she smiled. 'Rheumatics, you know.'

Gently Rachel took the old hands in hers.

'I think I remember you, Mrs Parker. There were so many, over the years, but I think I can place you,' she smiled.

'I've come to ask a great favour of you,' Rachel whispered. 'I want to find my daughter's mother—her natural mother. It means a great deal to me and I'm hoping you will help me.'

The elderly woman puckered her forehead into a frown then without speaking she took up her crochet again. Presently she said, without looking up,

'You realize what you are asking, Mrs Parker? You know that ethically it is impossible for me to help, even if I could.'

'You mean you *won't*?'

'Cannot, my dear. I've been retired these last ten

years and that's a long time. Even if it were possible to help I should need records, dates, times. I have none.'

'But you remember *me*?'

'Aye, I do, lassie. I do. But it's strange that we only seem to remember the good things. A body's inclined to put the bad bits and the sad bits from her mind. Likely I remember the joy of a woman being given a child to love, but it's wiser to try to forget the heartbreak of the one who gave that child up.'

A cold feeling gripped Rachel. It was starting all over again—the evasion, the reluctance to talk, the forgetting. Couldn't any of them realize how much it meant to Anne? Hadn't they the sense to see that it wasn't just idle curiosity that prompted her search?

'Miss McIver—*please*?' Rachel begged, her mouth dry with apprehension. 'Will you let me tell you why I want to find Anne's other mother? At least hear me out?'

'I'll listen, and gladly, but there's no way I can help you, much as I might think you should know.'

So yet again Rachel told her story and as if the old matron were her last hope, she told it with pleading in her voice, her eyes never leaving the time-worn face.

'You mean she gave the girl a hiding?' Matron interrupted as Rachel recounted the cause of Anne's moods, the start of it all, the day of the attack upon a classmate.

Rachel nodded and dropped her eyes for an instant.

'I know Anne shouldn't have done it,' she defended, 'but to have called her mother a tart—well, it upset her, got her on the raw; and look at the trouble it has caused.'

'Aye,' Matron sighed. 'Children can be very cruel, so they can. And your Anne gave the nasty wee besom a nose-bleed, eh? The lassie's got spunk!'

The faded eyes twinkled for an instant with a look that was strangely akin to pride.

'But I'm interrupting you—forgive me?'

Rachel felt a flood of gratitude towards Miss McIver, for it seemed that at last here was someone who understood and in understanding, might yet be persuaded to help. But she had not reckoned with the unbending, unassailable law that governs such matters, for even as she finished her story, even as she begged Anne's need to meet her natural mother, Rachel recognized that look on Matron McIver's face. She had seen it before as sadly James Whitaker shook his head. It was there as the brisk young matron had said,

'*I cannot help. I am not allowed to.*'

So it came as no shock when Miss McIver said,

'My dear, I have come across this need in adopted children many times in the past, but I just cannot tell you what you want to know.'

With despair coursing through her body like a dull pain, Rachel made one last desperate attempt.

'Matron! If I told you I seek this information on medical advice, if I offered to get you our doctor's signed statement that Anne really needs to meet her other mother, would you help me? *Please?*' she begged, tears of frustration welling in her eyes.

There was silence in the little room for a moment then Miss McIver held out her hands.

'Help me up, will you? Maybe there is something— only a little, you'll mind?'

Slowly and stiffly she made her way to the desk in the far corner, turning the tiny key with fumbling fingers. Carefully she removed six green, leatherbound books.

'My records,' she said, 'of my babies.'

She sighed and looked into Rachel's eyes.

'It never came to me to be a mother, so I did the next best thing. I trained as a midwife. And all the babies I helped into the world were *my* babies, Mrs Parker and so precious to me that I recorded all their births and some of the sad or happy things about them, too.'

She smiled gently. It was almost as if Rachel were no longer there; that the past had become the present and Matron's aching bones were young again. She opened the oldest-looking of the books.

'Wee Sandy,' she said. 'My first bairn. I was a young midwife then—with my own district for the first time alone. And Sandy was born in a slum tenement with borrowed blankets on the bed. He's a Chief Engineer, now, with a son at University.'

Rachel waited unspeaking, afraid to break the spell, as the old woman flicked through her books, each page a memory, the start of a little new life.

'And the last time—the last page—it was twin girls, Mrs Parker, born at the Home in Manchester, three days before I retired.'

She looked up and smiled, as though she had come to a decision.

'When was your Anne born, my dear?'

'September 7th, 1956,' Rachel whispered.

'Yes. Ah, yes.'

The old woman selected a book then slowly turned the pages.

'It was in the small, dark hours—they so often come then, I'll never know why—at ten minutes past two in the morning—to Rosemary, a daughter ...'

Tears pricked Rachel's eyes. Rosemary. Anne's mother

She repeated the name softly and it was almost as though she had always known it to be so.

'There's rosemary; that's for remembrance...'

The phrase came back mistily from her schooldays.

'Yes,' sighed Agnes McIver. 'Rosemary Jones from Morven. She was Welsh, I remember.'

'Morven?' Rachel breathed.

'In North Wales, she said it was. Ah, a pretty little thing—gentle...'

'And she cared, Matron? She wasn't a tart?'

'No, she was a good girl. Oh, she pretended not to care—mostly they all did—but I remember when she left the Home she went with me into the nursery for a last look at her baby. She bent down and kissed her then ran out, crying. I never saw her again.'

Rachel sniffed unashamedly and dabbed at her eyes. Then rose to her feet.

'Thank you for being so kind, Miss McIver. I won't keep you from your meal. You've been so good, so understanding. I can't tell you how grateful I am.'

The old lady smiled.

'Tell your Anne that her mother wasn't a tart, Mrs Parker. Tell her she was a gentle wee lassie. I know it's not much, the little I've been able to tell you—'

'But Miss McIver, you *have* helped me! I know her name, now, and the village she came from. I can start looking from there,'

'Oh, my dear,' Miss McIver's eyes looked earnestly into Rachel's and she shook her head pityingly. 'That wouldn't be her real name—oh, dear me, no! They never gave their real names or addresses—*never*. There's no Rosemary Jones, Mrs Parker and no Morven, be sure of that!'

FIVE

Daniel Steele knew something was very wrong the moment Rachel walked into the little parlour of the inn. Her face was paper-white and her eyes, as she searched the room for him, were wide with shock.

'Over here, Rachel!'

He used her name without thinking and she walked towards him, numbly.

'Hey! You look like you could use a drink,' he said, helping her into a chair.

'Please,' she whispered gratefully, fighting back the feeling of sick despair that throbbed in every pulse in her body.

When he put the brandy glass into her hand, Rachel took a large gulp. It snatched at her breath as she swallowed it but it seemed to warm away the chill hopelessness that had taken hold of her.

'I've asked the barmaid for some sandwiches for you,' Steele said with unaccustomed gentleness. 'Finish your drink then tell me what happened.'

Rachel did as she was told, glad of his presence. He was a safe person to be with—she had felt it last night, in his office. It amazed her that this time yesterday they had not even met yet somehow, for all his truculence, Rachel felt she had known Daniel Steele always. She drained her glass then said,

'I got a name and address out of Matron. I couldn't

believe my luck. It was all there, written down in one of her baby-books—kind of sentimental—Rosemary Jones, from Morven. Some little place in North Wales, she said it was,' Rachel shrugged, hesitating, willing her voice not to tremble or tears to spring to her eyes again.

'I felt over the moon until she told me it wasn't a real name. She said they never gave their real names or addresses, so there's no such place as Morven and no Rosemary Jones. We're back to square one, Mr Steele.'

'I see,' he retorted gravely. 'So what will you do now? Do you still want to go on with it?'

'Of course I do—but *how*?'

Steele stared into his glass. He felt sorry for Rachel Parker and it surprised him because he never let feelings interfere with business. But there was something about her—he couldn't quite fathom it—something feminine and appealing; an air of vulnerability. Suddenly he wanted very much to help her.

'The birth certificate? Had you thought of Somerset House?'

Rachel shook her head.

'No go. When the adoption became official we were given a completely new birth certificate, showing Anne to be our child. The original certificate—the *real* one—I never saw. Those certificates are kept in a special department within Somerset House. Nobody could get to see it, except under the most exceptional circumstances. That much I do know.'

'Hmm.' Steele shrugged. 'I suppose when I agreed to take this on, I knew there wasn't a lot of hope. You know, you're trying to breach the strongest, most watertight security wall there is. You realize that, don't you?'

They sat in moody silence for a while then Steele

said slowly,

'I reckon, though, that that's the worst of it. What about looking on the bright side?'

'Is there one?' Rachel whispered, bitterly.

'There could be. Just supposing Anne's mother had told the truth. What if there is a little place called Morven and that a Rosemary Jones lived there? And if you're looking for a bonus, who's to say she didn't go back there, after she left Manchester?'

Rachel gave a gasp of excitement.

'You really think she might have?'

'Hey! Calm down, now. It's only a shot in the dark, and it's our last chance,' he added, his voice warning her not to set her hopes too high.

'Are you game, then,' he asked, 'for one last try?'

'I'm game!' she smiled.

'Fine. Finish off your sandwich and I'll take you home—you've had enough for one day. Then I'll get on with checking on Morven—see if there really is such a place.'

'And if there is?'

'Then we're in business again, Mrs Parker!'

Rachel flopped on to the settee and kicked off her shoes. Daniel Steele had been right. She had had enough for one day, she thought as she plopped two aspirins into a glass and waited for the fizzing to stop.

She would sit for just a few minutes with her feet up, to give the tablets time to work, then she would take a long, hard look at the position to date and...

The ringing of the telephone awoke her with a start. She reached out for it, her hand unsteady.

'Three-nine-six-one,' she mumbled, blinking herself awake.

'Mum, you awful old stop-out! I've been trying to get you for ages. Where have you been?'

'Oh, here and there,' Rachel smiled, gladdened at the sound of her daughter's voice. 'Yesterday I went to Manchester and today I went to a little place called—'

She stopped, realizing that for the moment she dare not raise Anne's hopes too high.

'Well, never mind. Let's just say that I've been very busy on your behalf.'

'Oh, don't be so maddening, Mum. What have you found out?'

'W-e-l-l,' Rachel prevaricated, 'it's early days yet, but let's say I'm hopeful. In fact, I might be going to North Wales, pretty soon.'

'My other mother's Welsh? How did you find out? Are you going to see her?'

The excitement in Anne's voice was unmistakable, stressing afresh to Rachel how bitterly the young girl would be disappointed if things didn't go right—if they didn't find Rosemary.

'Hey there! Not so fast! I said *maybe*. Oh, Anne, it's a long story but I've got an Inquiry Agent on the job and he's following a lead. It's only a lead, mind.'

'A private eye? Gosh, Mum, you're a love, really you are! Oh, won't you tell me *anything*?'

'Not yet,' Rachel asserted firmly. 'You see, I can't be absolutely certain and I don't want you to be disappointed. But there's one thing I can tell you,' she hastened, eager to offer some small comfort. 'Your mother was a nice girl, that I know for sure, now. She cared about you, Anne. She cared a great deal.'

'Did she, Mum? Honestly?'

The young voice was wistful.

'Honestly.'

'And you *will* ring me and tell me, won't you, just as soon as you can? You've got Maggie's number?'

'Yes, I've got Maggie's number,' Rachel affirmed fondly. 'Now tell me, how are you, love? You sound so much brighter. And how's Maggie?'

'Oh, she's moaning about being cheated out of the wedding and she keeps on going on and on about Graham ...'

'And Maggie's right, too! Can't you meet Graham, Anne? Listen to what he's got to say. He loves you, you know.'

'Mum!' Anne's voice held an unspoken warning. 'You promised ...'

'Yes, I know, but—'

'Got to go, now,' Anne cut in and Rachel kicked herself mentally. She had vowed she would try not to mention Graham Hobson again—not until they had found Anne's other mother, anyway, yet as soon as the opportunity arose she was back on the old tack once more. But Anne was being so stubborn about Graham, Rachel fretted silently.

'Maggie and I are going to a disco. in town. I'll ring you tomorrow, and oh—I nearly forgot! What was that vicar's name—you know, the one at Manchester? Wasn't it Whitaker?'

'Yes. Why?'

'Well, it's a bit of a coincidence, I suppose, but I went into Dad's office this morning. I'd run out of tissues, you see, and I know he's always got a box somewhere around. Anyway, there was a note on his desk and I read it.'

'Now Anne,' Rachel admonished. 'You shouldn't have

done that! Now if Miss Tremlitt had been there...'

'Well, she wasn't and I know I shouldn't have, but somehow the name just seemed to jump up at me. The message was from the switchboard. It said that the Reverend James Whitaker had phoned and would Dad get in touch with him as soon as possible?'

'Mr Whitaker? From Manchester? You're sure, Anne?'

'Sure I'm sure. Don't you think you should ring him? He might have something to tell you.'

'But he rang Dad. Maybe it's private...'

'Well, he would, wouldn't he—ring Dad, I mean, if you've been out all day? And what's so private that you can't know about it?'

'W-e-ell,' Rachel conceded, doubtfully, 'I suppose you could be right.'

Something is wrong, she thought, apprehensively; something doesn't quite fit. Trying to keep her voice light and normal-sounding Rachel said,

'Did the telephonist put a time on the message, by any chance?'

'Yes, they always do. All messages are timed. It was 9.35 a.m. Why?'

'Oh, nothing. He'd be bound to ring Dad, I suppose, since I was out. I'll try to get hold of him—see what he wanted.'

But Rachel knew, even as she put the phone down, that she would not get in touch with James Whitaker. When she met him he had hedged and prevaricated and told her precisely nothing. Even last night when she phoned him from Daniel Steele's office, the only help he had given had been accidental and unknowing. Yet today Mr Whitaker had phoned John. Why had he done it? And, Rachel thought as apprehension grew inside her, why hadn't he telephoned Fair Oaks first? And he *hadn't* phoned, because at 9.35 this morning when the switchboard at Parker's had received the message, she had still been in, waiting for Steele to call. That call had come at 10.15—she had noted the time—and she had been in the house until nearly eleven o'clock. James Whitaker could have phoned her at home—had he really wanted to.

Rachel swallowed hard. She didn't like it. Something was very wrong and she didn't know what. She only knew that the old nagging in the pit of her stomach was back again and that suddenly she wanted very much to talk to Dan Steele.

For the second time that morning, Rachel impatiently replaced the phone, fretting that there was no reply from Daniel Steele's office yet all the time realizing that today was Sunday and like most men he was almost certainly at his home.

Home?

The sudden thought that Dan Steele had a home, a wife and children, even, was a sobering one. It surprised Rachel that she had never before thought of him as anything other than a slightly cynical, rather unkempt Inquiry Agent. But his after-office life was of no importance and she shrugged the thought away.

It was going to be a long, lonely day, she reflected, reluctantly admitting that it would be the morning at least before there was any more news. Yet perversely she was half glad about it, because if Miss McIver was right, if neither Rosemary Jones nor the village in which she had lived existed, at least for one more day, she could put off telling Anne that the search they started so hopefully had ended.

Wandering into the summer-room, she took the long-spouted watering can and tried to interest herself in the plants, removing a dead leaf here, an unwanted shoot there, debating whether or not to phone John in Holland. But she didn't usually ring her husband when he was away on business and if she were to do it today, he might ask her what she had been doing. She would have to lie to him then and she didn't want to do that, not even for Anne's sake. Nor, she thought, could she break the frustration of the day by phoning Anne. Anne was too tense, was hoping for too much, too quickly. Not for her the possibility that they might never be able to find her other mother—that unknown woman who had kissed her child gently then left her at the Home in Manchester.

Startled, Rachel realized that never before had she thought of the first moment of Anne's being, had never wondered if she were the child of a sweet and tender love or if her begetting had been of no more consequence than the burning passion of two people, briefly met and quickly parted.

Oh, let them have loved, she prayed silently. Let them have cared for each other.

Impatiently she set down the can. Usually, just to be in the green-filled summer-room soothed and calmed her, but today she was restless, feeling annoyance that a precious day was being wasted. On Friday, John would be home again and he would ask—no, he would demand —that she stop the search for Anne's other mother. And when he did that, Rachel thought with a shudder, she dared not begin to imagine what the outcome would be.

She tilted her chin and impatiently tossed back her long, black hair. It was almost ten o'clock yet she was still mooning around in dressing-gown and slippers. She needed company, someone to talk to.

Joyce Lee, her subconscious supplied. Joyce always understood.

'Bill not in?' Rachel asked when half an hour later she was seated in the cosy, well-used kitchen of her doctor's home.

'Gone fishing,' Joyce Lee supplied, not troubling to disguise the relief in her voice, 'and taken the boys with him.'

Deftly she shaped the top of an apple pie, her thumb and forefinger pinching round the edge methodically.

'How's it going, then?' she asked without raising her eyes. 'John still laying down the law, is he?'

'Yes,' Rachel nodded. 'He phoned from Rotterdam on Thursday and warned me off. Oh, it was very gently done, but there was no mistaking it. There'll be trouble when he gets back and finds out, nothing is so certain.'

'But you'll still go on with it?'

'I've got to. And what have I found out, do you suppose? Only that Anne's mother might be called Rosemary Jones and she might have come from North Wales.'

'How do you know that?'

'Oh. Daniel Steele found out—not me. He's my only hope now, truth known ...'

And as Joyce Lee placed the last of the pies to bake and filled up the coffee percolator, Rachel told her of the hopeless visit to Manchester, the desperation that drove her to seek Steele's help and of the ever-nagging fear of what failure would do to Anne.

'Sometimes I think I was a fool ever to have started it,' Rachel sighed, bitterly. 'John's against it, yet Anne is determined to meet her other mother. It's a case of the devil or the deep blue sea. I don't have much of a choice, do I?'

'My, but it's a terrible life,' Joyce Lee agreed soberly. Then she grinned. 'Heck! Let's live dangerously! Be blowed to the coffee. How's about a nice gin and tonic, uh? Won't cure your ailments, old love, but it's sure nicer than medicine,' she chuckled wickedly.

Two hours and three drinks later, Rachel walked home feeling better for Joyce's cheerful company and the medicinal effect of mid-morning gin on an empty stomach.

'I will not worry,' she whispered. 'Worrying brings on wrinkles. Leave it all to Steele—after all, that's what I'm paying him for.'

She pointed her latch-key at the front door lock and was relieved that it found its mark at the first attempt.

Good old Joyce, she thought as she kicked off her shoes and padded into the kitchen in search of coffee. The bright red extension-phone that sat silently in the kitchen invited her to ring Steele's office yet again. For a moment she hesitated, finger poised, then shrugging her shoulders, replaced the receiver.

'But what is he *doing*?' she fretted. 'When will he phone? Doesn't he realize how little time there is?'

Daniel Steele sniffed suspiciously at the half-empty bottle of milk then decided to drink his coffee black and sweet.

'Morvedd,' he muttered, flicking through the small

red book of dialling codes.

There was no Morven in the gazetteer he had borrowed from his obliging police-sergeant friend, but there had been a Morvedd. It had only needed a deceptively simple call to Directory Enquiries,

'Give me the number of Morvedd Post Office, will you, please?'

The longest of long-shots paying off.

'Post Office, Morvedd. It's Sunday and we're closed!' announced a female voice, richly Welsh. But closed or not, its owner had not put down the phone, because when he wanted, Daniel Steele had a soft, persuasive way with him that was hard to resist. He apologized profusely, hoping he hadn't interrupted the cooking of her Sunday joint, knowing how busy she must be, but if she could spare him just a few moments ... ?

He was looking for a Miss Jones, he said. He and his wife particularly wanted to get in touch with her. It would be their silver wedding, soon, and they thought it would be a nice time to bring together all their long-ago friends.

Nothing could have appealed more to the romantic heart of the postmistress of Morvedd.

'Well, that's nice,' she cooed. 'Now which Jones will it be? Jones the Shop, Jones the Milk?'

'Rosemary Jones,' Steele hazarded. 'She was a friend of my wife's.'

'Rosemary, eh? Now that'll be Jones Police's daughter. But they've been left Morvedd a long time. There were two girls, if I remember rightly—Mair and Rosemary. P.C. Jones got killed you know, by a hit-and-run driver and Mrs Jones died not long after. Very sad, that was.'

'And what happened to the daughters?'

'Well, Mair got married to an Englishman, I believe and Rosemary went nursing. Your wife's a nurse is she Mr er—'

'Steele,' came the prompt reply. 'Yes, Rachel's a nurse—or was. But can you tell me anything more, ma'am? You don't know where Rosemary—or Mair —went after they left Morvedd?'

'Sorry, no. But Llew Price might know, Mr Steele. He wrote to Rosemary for ever so long. I know that for a fact. If you were to get in touch with Llew, now, he'd maybe be able to help you. He was the schoolmaster here—retired, these five years. Lives at Nantwood Cottage—I could give you his phone number, if you'd like to give him a ring.'

Steele thanked her, but even as he wrote down the number she gave him he knew he had no intention of announcing his arrival in Morvedd. An unheralded visit would be best, he decided; the personal touch and all that.

So, he reflected triumphantly, replacing the phone, Anne Parker's mother had told the truth. There *was* a Rosemary Jones who once lived in Morvedd. Now, if their luck held, the schoolmaster might at least be able to remember the hospital to which he sent the letters. And if Lady Luck really smiled on them, he might soon be on Rosemary's trail.

But that was all pie in the sky. All he could tell Rachel Parker was that Rosemary Jones might be genuine, that she had left Morvedd to become a nurse and might, if she had qualified, have a registration number that could be traced.

Picking up the phone, he dialled Rachel's number.

'How about a quick trip to Wales?' he asked without ceremony.

Rachel's delighted cry pleased him.

'You've found it? There really is a Morven?'

'No, Matron got it wrong. It's Morvedd—pronounced Morveth—but Rosemary Jones lived there, once.'

He broke off abruptly.

'Look, we're wasting time. Just give me an hour and I'll be with you. O.K.?'

'Oh, yes! Just as soon as you like,' Rachel gasped. 'How on earth did you manage it?'

'Tell you later,' Steele replied, tantalizingly. 'See you.'

Rachel put down the phone and took a deep breath. She was light-headed enough without this news; better make herself a quick sandwich. She'd have time wouldn't she? And what should she wear? Steele had sounded elated, almost as if this time he was really on to something. Her stomach was giving funny little skips of excitement and she laughed aloud from sheer joy. The sun was shining and it was a lovely day for a visit to Wales —the most beautiful day on which to look for Rosemary!

'You know, Mr Steele, I should be very cross with you—telling such awful lies,' Rachel smiled, leaning back in her seat, contentment washing over her.

'And just how far would the truth have got me?' Steele demanded, his eyes on the road ahead. 'Tell them you are looking for a girl who had an illegitimate baby in Manchester and you'll get nowhere. They clam up, those country people—protect their own. Besides, Rosemary Jones probably didn't want them to know in Morvedd about the baby. It wouldn't have been right, would it, to let it out? Now, a silver wedding; that's something different,' he grinned unashamedly, 'and when we meet this schoolmaster, remember you're supposed to have been married to me for nearly twenty-five years, will you? Don't go calling me Mr Steele, uh? And you were a nurse with Rosemary, too, don't forget that either.'

'And where were we supposed to have done our training, me and Rosemary?'

'I don't know, yet. You'll have to leave that to me to find out. We'll just play it by ear ...'

Rachel glanced sideways yet again at Daniel Steele. Something had happened to him. He smelled of aftershave and his hair had been trimmed. Add to that a tweed suit, checked shirt and mohair tie and he looked, heaven help her Rachel thought, almost human.

He turned and smiled briefly.

'Well? Do you think you could try to act like my ever-loving? Could you force yourself to call me Dan?'

'I think I might try,' Rachel whispered, furious with herself for blushing like a girl on her first date, 'but I think I like Daniel best ...'

'Okay, Rachel,' Steele smiled again. 'Daniel it is!'

Somewhere in the back of Rachel's mind a small uneasy voice whispered a warning, but she ignored it. The day was sweet and warm; they were going to Wales to see a man who knew Rosemary. It was not a day for caution!

SIX

It came as no surprise to Llewelyn Price when a car bearing a Birmingham registration stopped outside his home. He had already been well briefed by Dilys-Post Office.

'... Said he wanted to find Rosemary Jones,' she told him only that morning at Chapel. 'You'll remember the Jones girls, Llew? Well, he seemed very nice—name of Steele. Hope you didn't mind my telling him about you?'

The elderly schoolmaster hadn't minded at all. His wife was at Betws-y-Coed for the weekend at her sister's place and a visitor from England would make a welcome break in his lonely day. And he was glad he had set a tea-tray in readiness with the rosebud china, since it seemed apparent that the gentleman had brought his wife along, too.

'Good day to you,' he smiled as he opened the door to Steele's knock. 'You're not entirely unexpected, you know. News travels fast, in Morvedd.'

'You'll have some idea why we're here, then?' Rachel smiled, pleased by their welcome.

'You're looking for Rosemary? Yes, I heard. But come you in, Mrs Steele. I can't tell you much—it's a long time since the Jones girls left Morvedd—but we might as well make ourselves comfortable, eh?'

His simple kindness made Rachel squirm. She didn't

really like masquerading as Steele's wife, but she had little choice. To have told the complete truth to Mr Price would have betrayed Rosemary, and they couldn't do that.

The old man settled himself in an armchair.

'They were nice folk, the Jones family, very close and affectionate. After Constable Jones died, his wife just seemed to give up living. I suppose there's a fancy medical name for it, but folks in these parts reckoned she died of a broken heart. The girls left Morvedd shortly afterwards. There's not a lot here for young people. Mair had met her Englishman by then and Rosemary decided to go nursing. We tried to do all we could for them, my wife and I—*in loco parentis*, you might say.'

'And you kept in touch?' Steele asked. 'You know where they are, still?'

Llewelyn Price shook his head.

'It was Rosemary who wrote regularly. I didn't hear much from Mair. Came from some place in Yorkshire, Mair's letters, but I forget now, from where,' he said, apologetically. 'It must be nearly twenty years ago, you know.'

'It doesn't matter, Mr Price,' Rachel smiled. 'It's Rosemary we really want to find.'

'Ah, now. Rosemary and I wrote to each other for nearly two years,' the old man nodded. 'A bright girl she was. If her parents had lived they'd have seen her through University, that's for sure. A great pity,' he said, half to himself.

Rachel glowed inwardly. Here was something else to tell Anne. Rosemary had been clever—university material, in fact.

'And then?' Steele prompted as the old man lapsed into memories.

'Well, suddenly Rosemary's letters stopped, Mr Steele. It mystified me, I can tell you. It just wasn't like Rosemary. I wrote once or twice more but someone returned my letters. *Gone away*, they were marked and *Return to Sender*. It was all very sad.'

'That would be when she was nursing?'

'That's it, Mr Steele. At Manchester. Quite a few girls from these parts have gone to Manchester hospitals, you know.'

Rachel drew sharply on her breath as she felt a small stab of alarm. Manchester. It seemed that all roads led to Manchester and ended abruptly at a blank brick wall.

'But you would know that, Mrs Steele?'

'Yes—er—yes,' Rachel floundered. Then she recovered sufficiently to say,

'But Rosemary and I only worked together—we had different digs.'

It was an ambiguous statement, flung out on the spur of the moment.

'Oh, I see. Then you aren't the young lady she shared a bed-sitter with? You're not Sylvia?'

'No, Mr Price. I'm Rachel,' she returned, glad of the unwitting prompt he had given her. 'I lived in the Nurses' Home. Rosemary preferred to live out. Funny, but I can't remember where it was.'

She was lying through her teeth and she hated it, the more so since Mr Price was such a nice, gentle old man. But Steele was looking at her approvingly and the end, she supposed, would justify the means. Anne was the only person who mattered, and anyway, they were white lies, weren't they? Or maybe only slightly grey ... ?

'Ah, now there I can help you,' Mr Price beamed. 'I'm an old hoarder, my wife always says. Threatens regularly every spring-clean to throw out my rubbish, you know,' he chuckled. 'I've still got Rosemary's last address, I'm almost sure of it.'

For a moment he rummaged amongst the contents of a cluttered desk then straightened up with a grunt of triumph.

'Here it is! My old address book.'

He dipped into his pocket and settled his glasses on his nose.

'Yes, here we are—Rosemary's Manchester address. I'll copy it down for you, Mrs Steele. You never know, it might be a help to you.'

'I'm sure it will,' Steele retorted, 'and if not, maybe the hospital people could help us. We should have thought of them,' he said, with studied unconcern, as if they had known all along the hospital at which Rosemary once worked.

'Yes, indeed,' smiled Llewelyn Price, 'but we don't always think, do we?'

He handed Steele a small piece of card on which he had written an address in old-fashioned writing, firm and flowing.

'It's not a lot, but I've been pleased to give you what help I could. I suppose you wouldn't like a cup of tea? We always have one about this time, when my wife is at home.'

'We'd like one very much, wouldn't we darling?' came Steele's prompt reply, eager for an excuse to stay longer.

'If it wouldn't be too much trouble?' Rachel faltered,

fixing Steele with a warning look.

'You don't have to overdo it,' she whispered when they were alone.

'I know, but I can't resist it; you blush so very prettily, Rachel,' he grinned.

And because she liked Daniel Steele better when he wasn't being tight-lipped and curt; because at last it seemed they had found something that might help them, she smiled back, hopeful for the first time.

They had barely closed the garden gate behind them before Rachel gasped.

'Isn't it wonderful? For the first time we've really got something to go on!'

Her eyes were shining, her cheeks flushed.

'Where do you suppose we should go first? The hospital or the digs?'

'Hold on!' Steele retorted indulgently. 'All we've got is an address.'

'But it's a start, surely?'

Steele switched on the ignition and put the car into gear.

'Is it? What do you really expect to find at Rosemary's old lodgings? She shared a bed-sitter with another nurse called Sylvia, twenty years ago. It's odds-against that anybody living there now will remember her. Why, the house might even be gone. Could have been pulled down, for all we know.'

His words had the effect of a douche of ice-cold water, flung with deliberate unconcern into Rachel's face.

Stiff-lipped she retorted, 'Well, there's the hospital.'

'*Which* hospital?'

'Damn!' Rachel jerked petulantly. 'We didn't find

out!'

'No, and thank heaven you didn't try to! You were nursing once with Rosemary Jones—remember? You'd have known the hospital, wouldn't you?'

Rachel closed her eyes.

'I'm an idiot, aren't I?'

'Yes, but a well-meaning one, if I may say so.'

'You may,' Rachel whispered, 'but it doesn't help any. I'd do a lot better if I stopped to think, instead of jumping in with both feet all the time, wouldn't I?'

The despondency in her voice was unmistakable. She seemed to Daniel Steele like a small, disappointed child. Gently he covered her hand with his.

'Listen now, don't get upset. We're not finished yet, but it's going to take time. We've got an address and it's going to help us when we start checking round the hospitals.'

'And there are quite a few in Manchester, aren't there?' Rachel acknowledged, dully.

Steele nodded.

'But there's the Nursing Register, remember, and the Health and Social Security people. They might be able to help. And what about the Salvation Army? They're very good at finding missing people.'

He have her hand a little squeeze before releasing it. 'So cheer up, eh?'

'And what story do we tell them this time? Will we be still on the silver wedding tack or am I to be Mair Jones looking for my long-lost sister?'

Steele recognized the despair in her voice and tears that were not very far away. He said seriously,

'No Rachel, we'll have to tell the truth—at least to the Social Security people and the Salvation Army, if we decide to approach them. It's up to you, though, what line you take at Manchester. I take it you'll be going to Manchester tomorrow?'

'Of course I'll be going. Won't you?'

'No, I'm sorry, but I can't. Tomorrow I'm a witness in a divorce case. It's a defended action and I'll most likely be tied up in court all day—maybe even Tuesday, as well.'

'Oh, I see,' she shrugged, her disappointment evident. She had come to look upon the two of them as something of a team. She should have realized Steele must have other irons in the fire. But John would be back soon, and time was running out. She would have to go alone to Manchester.

'Well, I shouldn't have expected anything else, should I? All the lies we told to Mr Price, I mean. I don't deserve any luck, do I?'

Steele stared straight ahead of him, concentrating on the country road that was little more than a lane.

'It hurts you doesn't it Rachel—telling untruths? You see things as either black or white; there's no inbetweens, for you. You're an all-or-nothing-person, aren't you?'

'I suppose so,' she hesitated, dubiously.

'Yet you're going on with this, in spite of the fact that your husband has forbidden it?'

'My husband,' came the icy retort, 'doesn't *forbid* me to do anything, Mr Steele.'

'*Daniel*, uh? Don't you think we could keep it up for just a little longer? You see, I'd hoped we might make a day of it. There's a good pub not far from here. We could stop for a meal—a little celebration?'

'Is there something to celebrate?'

Her reply was more curt than she had intended.

'Yes, Rachel, I think there is, but gently does it. We know that Anne's mother was called Rosemary Jones—still might be—and that she lived in the police house in Morvedd. We know she was a nurse in Manchester and that the letters stopped coming to Mr Price about twenty years ago. I think we've found the right Rosemary. I think we might allow ourselves a little celebration, Rachel.'

'So you don't think it's utterly hopeless?'

'No, I don't, but you've got to learn to be patient—Anne, too. As far as I can see, it's going to be a long and tedious job.'

'And even then I have to face the fact we might not be lucky?'

'Maybe even then. Take the Salvation Army, for instance. If they did trace Rosemary, they wouldn't tell you, Rachel. Not right away.'

'Why not?'

Rachel jerked her head to meet Steele's eyes in the driving mirror.

'Why shouldn't they tell me?'

'Because first they'd be morally bound to tell Rosemary. They would have to first be sure that she wanted to meet Anne. You see, Rosemary could be married now, with a husband who may know nothing of what happened in Manchester. Had you thought of that, Rachel?'

'Yes, I had. I think of it all the time. But surely she couldn't refuse me? I'd promise to be discreet, not make any trouble. And I'd make Anne promise, too.'

'Well, let's worry about that when and if it happens. We've done enough for one day. It's half-past six and I'm hungry. Relax, Rachel. Let's have that meal at The Feathers, uh? Strictly business, of course.'

He asked it hesitantly, a strange shyness in his voice that didn't seem one bit like the Daniel Steele she had first met, Rachel pondered. It would be churlish of her to refuse, wouldn't it, because it seemed he had planned it all along. He had gone to obvious trouble with his appearance—the hair cut alone must have been no small feat of endurance to a man like Steele. And why shouldn't they have a meal together? Like he said, it was strictly business.

'Now that you mention it, I'm hungry, too. Therefore *Daniel*,' mischievously she emphasized his name, 'I would be happy to have dinner with you—strictly business, strictly dutch, of course.'

'We'll haggle about the bill later,' he grunted as the car gathered speed. 'Not too far to go—just a couple of miles up the road ...'

He stared ahead, concentrating on the narrow, twisting road. He didn't speak again, but when their eyes met in the driving mirror, he smiled happily. He was almost handsome when he smiled, Rachel thought. Pity he didn't do it more often ...

The Feathers had once been an out-of-the-way country inn, but an enterprising new landlord had at once recognized the potential of its stone-built quaintness and the wild, beautiful scenery in which it was set. Now, with the acquisition of a London-trained chef and head waiter, it was easily the most popular eating place for miles around.

On the surface of it, nothing had been changed and concessions to modern-day comfort were cleverly disguised. Old-fashioned oil paintings of shire horses, cows and dogs were clustered on the uneven, white-washed walls and logs crackled in a wide stone fireplace. Copper and brass glinted everywhere and jugs of spring blossom stood on the wide window-sills.

'It's beautiful,' Rachel breathed, glad she had come.

'Food's good, too,' Steele retorted gruffly, trying not to look pleased at her pleasure.

A waiter handed them menus and asked if they would like a drink. Remembering the medicinal gin of Joyce Lee's early morning prescribing, Rachel intended to refuse but was not surprised to hear herself asking for a sherry as Steele ordered a large dry Martini.

'Cheers!' he said, lifting his glass.

'To Rosemary!' Rachel replied, gravely.

Steele nodded then said briskly,

'Right! This was supposed to be a business dinner but let's be devils. Let's talk about other things—'

'Like?'

'Oh, ships and shoes and sealing-wax and...'

'Wives,' Rachel interrupted, briskly. 'Tell me about your wife, Daniel, and your family.'

Tell me, she thought, about the woman who doesn't bother to sew on your shirt buttons or care that you seem to spend the better part of your day away from home.

For a moment Steele hesitated, twirling the stem of his glass reflectively as if he were composing a straight answer to a straight question.

'Her name is Elaine,' he said, tersely. 'She's a secretary to the Sales Director of a big company. Mike, our son, is at Leicester University and our daughter, Julia, was married last August. If I remember rightly, Elaine and I acted in a very civilized manner on that occasion ...'

He broke off, his voice curt and tired, Rachel thought, like the night she had walked despairingly into his shabby little office.

'It was quite an effort, all things considered. We did it for Julia, I suppose.'

He raised his eyes and looked directly into Rachel's.

'Elaine and I were divorced three years ago,' he said simply.

'Oh, Daniel—I'm so sorry. Your private life should be no business of mine,' Rachel said, hastily. 'I shouldn't have asked—I had no right ...'

'Maybe not, but it doesn't bother me now. We agreed on the divorce in a calm and sensible manner—breakdown of the marriage and all that,' he shrugged. 'I was only a part-time husband and father, truth known. My police work came first—always did. No woman is going to play second fiddle to that.'

He shrugged again then said softly,

'We sold up the home—made a completely new start. Elaine has a flat in town, now, and I've got a place near the office. I left the police force, of course—set up on my own. Better that way ...'

'Look, there's no need to explain anything,' Rachel broke in, her cheeks burning, her eyes downcast. 'It was rude of me to ask and I feel awful about it. You wouldn't have asked such a question of *me*.'

'No, I suppose not and I won't, either. There's no to need to. I can read you like an open book, Rachel.'

Her eyes jerked up, warily.

'Read out aloud, then,' she challenged, feeling that maybe it was her turn now, for punishment.

Steele drained his glass then set it down slowly before

answering.

'For some reason,' he said quietly, 'you're jumpy as a kitten. You have a daughter you love—too much for her own good and a husband who has made it to the top in record time. Your home—what I've seen of it—borders on luxury and you seem to lack nothing. So what's gone wrong with *your* marriage, Rachel?'

'What do you mean,' she whispered, her lips stiff and her mouth suddenly dry. 'There's nothing wrong with my marriage.'

'No? Then why are you so sad—yes, you *are* sad,' he hastened. 'Often you look lost and lonely and there's a look of bewilderment about you sometimes that makes me want to—'

'I'm not in the least bewildered,' Rachel retorted, trying to smile, to make light of his remark. 'I know precisely what I'm doing, thanks just the same.'

'Then why are you apprehensive? Yes, I think apprehensive is the right word. It's as if you're waiting for something to happen. Or is it because your husband doesn't approve of what you are doing, Rachel? Why are you defying him? Why are you trying to find Anne's mother in spite of his wishes?'

Rachel shifted uncomfortably and fingered the napkin on her side-plate.

'I'm not defying him—well, not exactly,' she hedged, her eyes on her fingers. 'It's just that men don't feel the same way as women; they don't understand. And as for my marriage—well, we're not exactly in the first flush of wedded bliss. We've had our silver wedding, you know ...'

'All right, Rachel. You don't have to defend yourself. Don't protest too much ...'

A waiter coughed behind them and Steele started.

'Sorry,' he said. 'Give us a couple of minutes, will you?'

He handed Rachel a menu.

'The steak is good here,' he said when the waiter had left them, turning off their conversation as if it had been of no consequence, 'and the pâté is the chef's speciality. Pâté and steak suit you?'

Rachel nodded, dumbly. Steele seemed to know The Feathers well. Had he come here with Elaine or was there some other woman, now?

She shrugged. Did it matter? Tomorrow she would go to Manchester—alone. She would find out where Rosemary was and with luck there would be no more need for Dan Steele's help after that. She would pay his fully-detailed account and that would be the end of his blunt, disturbing ways.

'Okay, Rachel?'

His voice invaded her thoughts and she blushed guiltily.

'Yes please. Whatever you say,' she replied quickly.

His eyes held hers, asking silently that they should enjoy the evening and she smiled gently, understanding completely.

Signalling to the waiter, Steele gave their orders as somewhere in the background, music began to play.

Rachel fidgeted with the clasp of her handbag and tried not to think about John. She had been trying not to think about him for the best part of the day, if she were honest. And it wasn't as if she felt anything for Steele—nothing more than curiosity, she supposed, and now that she knew him better, pity that his life was in such a mess.

But there was an air of intrigue about tonight. She was a married woman and she had no right to be sitting at an intimately-lit table with another man, not even if it meant nothing more than a strictly business, strictly dutch affair.

All things considered, then, should she be enjoying herself quite so much, finding she liked that side of Daniel Steele's nature he had been so careful to keep to himself?

'Do you dance, Rachel?'

She nodded and Steele rose to his feet, holding out his hand to her, taking her arm, leading her on to the floor.

'It's a long time since I danced,' he smiled, half apologetically.

How long? Rachel wondered. Way back, perhaps, when he and Elaine were still together?

The floor was small, allowing only for gentle, intimate dancing; the music was soft and slow and throbbing.

I shouldn't be doing this, Rachel thought. Four days ago I didn't even know Dan Steele existed, yet now we are dining and dancing in a dimly-lit atmosphere as if it's all very right and proper. And it isn't at all right, her conscience nagged because when something is vaguely wrong with a woman's marriage, when she is restless and uneasy and unable to talk it out with her husband, then it is unwise to feel an inexplicable sense of safeness in the company of a near-stranger. And she had felt that way with Dan Steele, right from the first moment of their meeting.

'Relax,' Steele said softly in her ear. 'I'm not going to spoil your best shoes, or anything.'

He emphasized the word anything as if to imply

that even her reputation would be quite safe with him.

'Sorry,' Rachel whispered, blushing, 'but I don't usually do this, you know.'

Oh, why couldn't she be cool about it all, and sophisticated? Why was she so lacking in aplomb, so naïve?

'I know, Rachel,' Steele laughed indulgently, 'that's very obvious, but supposing, since you *are* doing it, that you try to enjoy yourself. Just take it easy,' he coaxed. 'It's all right ...'

Then he smiled down at her as he felt the tension leave her body.

Steele was quite right, Rachel thought. What harm could there possibly be in a meal and a few dances?

She leaned closer to him and felt again the strength of his body, the safeness of his encircling arm. She needed that strength so much and for just a little while, she would take it. Tomorrow it might all be over, their business at an end and on Friday, anyway, John would be back.

She shut out all thoughts of John quite deliberately because Dan's cheek had come to rest on hers and the music was in waltz-time and soft and sensuous.

She whispered, half-heartedly,

'We're enjoying this far too much, you know. You and I are supposed to be an old married couple—remember?'

She did not attempt to pull away from him.

'Indeed I do, Mrs Steele,' he said, his voice rough. 'Indeed I do ...'

His arms tightened about her.

This is mad, Rachel thought. It is quite, quite mad. It did not surprise her that suddenly, she did not care.

SEVEN

Rachel stood in the open doorway and held up her hand in a brief salute. In the waiting car, Daniel Steele flicked his headlights in acknowledgment then drove slowly down the drive and into the dark, deserted road.

With a sigh that was part relief, part regret, Rachel pushed home the bolts and slipped the door-chain into position.

'Shall I come in for a minute while you have a quick look round?' Steele had asked as they stopped outside Fair Oaks. 'It's my copper's training,' he smiled, 'but it *is* late and you're all alone.'

His concern had touched her but no, she said, it would be all right—if he would just wait for a few minutes?

It had been churlish not to ask him in she supposed, when it had been such a wonderful day; the finding of someone who had known Anne's mother, the discovery that Rosemary Jones really existed, the address that might help them in their search. And afterwards, at the little country inn, the candlelight and the slow, sweet music they danced to. She had allowed herself to unwind in Dan Steele's company. Truth known, she conceded flatly, she had enjoyed herself too well.

Strange, she mused, but as they had danced they spoke very little. Their talk was of trivialities, like two people meeting for the first time, discovering each other.

And had it been wholly by chance they had not mentioned either Elaine or John again?

Rachel shrugged and unbuttoned her coat, stuffing her gloves into the pockets. The piece of paper Dan had given her was still there.

'Let me know how you get on in Manchester, won't you, Rachel? If there's no reply from the office, it's almost certain I'll be at my place. You'll easily find it. First left then second on the right—just a couple of streets away.'

He had written down his home address—just in case.

Rachel tried hard not to wish he could be going with her to Manchester, hoping the court hearing he was attending would only last a day and not drag on and on. But if she cared to admit it, she had come to depend upon Daniel Steele, she admitted uneasily. At first she hadn't much liked him or his brusque manner and then she had come to feel pity for the mess his life was in, for his obvious loneliness and his broken marriage. Now she was beginning to think of him as a friend; a friend who danced well, who knew of small, intimate inns and who worried in case she was afraid to be alone all night.

She took a deep, impatient breath. She was being extremely foolish and all because he had treated her gently at a time when she was feeling fragile and neglected. She was employing him to find Rosemary Jones, she told herself firmly, and their relationship was a business one.

The telephone broke into her uneasy thoughts with a welcome purr.

'Mum! Where on earth have you been? I've been ringing all night!'

'Anne, love! It's past midnight. You should be in bed.'

Desperately Rachel tried to order her scattered thoughts.

'I know I should, but I've been waiting up for you. You said you'd ring. Where have you been until now?'

The voice was anxious and accusing.

'Hey! Steady on there. Your mother's a big girl, now!'

'Sorry Mum. You know I didn't mean anything, but I've been waiting and wondering all day.'

Rachel felt a flush of guilt.

'Yes, I do see, but you mustn't get over anxious, not at this stage. After all, it's early days yet.'

'Then you didn't find anything?'

The disappointment in Anne's voice was evident.

'Yes, we did as a matter of fact. We were quite lucky really, but—'

'But *what*? Why won't you tell me? Why are you stalling?'

'I'm not stalling,' Rachel replied firmly as she heard the tears trembling ominously in her daughter's voice. Anne was getting far too tense. Soon she would make herself ill if she continued worrying so. Wasn't there the shop-lifting affair to prove it? Rachel thought apprehensively.

'Listen,' she said more gently, 'there just *might* be good news for you—but tomorrow. Remember I said I'd be going to Wales? Well, that's where I've been.'

Deliberately she pushed all thoughts of the little inn from her mind.

'... and I spoke to someone there who knew your mother.'

'*You did?* Oh, where is she now?'

'I don't know, Anne, but I got her last-known address, so we've made a start, haven't we? And there's something else I'll tell you,' she continued placatingly. 'We know her name. She was called Rosemary Jones and she had a sister called Mair.'

There was a little gasp of delight then Anne whispered,

'Rosemary? *Rosemary* ...'

She repeated the name gently, caressing each syllable.

'You're sure? You wouldn't make it up, Mum? You wouldn't lie to me?'

'No, Anne, it's the truth, but that's all I'm going to tell you now, except that I'm going to Manchester again in the morning and you can't come with me,' she added, hurriedly anticipating Anne's thoughts.

'Oh, all right—but isn't it funny, Mum—us once living in Manchester, too? Do you think she'll still be there—Rosemary, I mean ... ?'

All tenseness seemed to have left Anne now and there was excitement in her voice. She was up and down, Rachel thought, like a yo-yo.

'Sorry, but that's all I'm going to tell you,' Rachel forced herself to speak lightly, 'so you can go to bed now and just be patient. And I'm going to bed, too. I'm tired!'

Blowing a kiss into the phone, Rachel replaced the receiver with a hand that trembled. Oh, she just *had* to be lucky tomorrow. So much depended on it—so very much.

Sleep didn't come easily to Rachel for all her weariness, for she knew how slender were the chances that there would still be someone at the address who remembered Rosemary and her one-time flatmate, Sylvia. Like Daniel had warned, she fretted, tossing in the big, empty bed, who was to say that even the house remained. Those big, old places were being bought up by builders for the sake of the generous gardens on which they stood; gardens that could take four or even six little new houses.

If only Daniel were going with her, Rachel wished into the darkness, she would feel better about it. She wanted him with her so much.

Ashamed, she reached out and touched the empty pillow beside her; John's pillow. In a little more than three days he would be back from Rotterdam and then what?

Resolutely Rachel squeezed her eyes tight shut, but it was too late, for already tears of utter misery were running unchecked down her cheeks.

Rachel crossed her fingers for good luck then once more glancing at the paper on which Llewelyn Price had written Rosemary's address, she walked resolutely down the wide, tree-lined road in north Manchester. She had expected at the best that the house would be a neglected shambles of bed-sits and that at the worst it would have vanished completely, yet here it stood, No. 17, the well-tended property of obviously prosperous owners. Its large windows were white-painted, the shutters and front door were a deep, rich blue, and it stood amid flowering trees and beds of tulips and wallflowers. Relieved beyond all measure, Rachel read the brass plate on the stone gatepost.

C. V. Carson. F.R.C.S.

It seemed like an omen, she thought hopefully. Once, two young nurses lived in one of its rooms and now it belonged to a surgeon. Oh, surely she would be lucky today?

The door was opened immediately she rang the bell.

'Hullo. Did you want Mr Carson?'

'No. Well, that is—I'm not sure,' Rachel mumbled, taken aback by the unexpectedly friendly greeting.

The woman who stood in the open doorway was, she supposed, about her own age—maybe a little younger.

She was dressed in bright red slacks and a white sweater and her brightly-painted toe nails peeped out from wooden-soled sandals.

'I'm Mrs Carson. Did you have an appointment? I'm afraid my husband's at the hospital all day.'

She grinned engagingly.

'But do come in—I've just brewed up and I don't much like drinking alone. I'm sure you could do with a cuppa and I could do with a bit of company.'

'Oh, thank you,' Rachel breathed. 'I've just arrived from Birmingham and I didn't get anything on the train.'

'Birmingham? You're not a patient, then?'

'No, Mrs Carson. As a matter of fact, I've come to ask a favour and I think you might be better able to help me than your husband.'

'Hmm. Go on. Sounds intriguing—it's a long way to come to ask a favour.'

She led the way into a small sitting-room.

'Now, sit down and I'll get another cup. Then you can tell me what it's all about.'

'You'll not laugh at me, Mrs Carson?' Rachel asked

when they were comfortably settled. 'You see, what I'm trying to do is so crazy ... I'm looking for two young nurses who once lived here—twenty years ago.'

The other woman set down her cup, a quizzical expression settling on her face, her mouth quirking at the corners as if she were trying not to smile.

'Go on,' she urged. 'Try me. Who were they, these long-ago nurses? What were they called?'

Rachel smiled back then said, ruefully,

'Sylvia and Rosemary and they had a bed-sitter at this address—or so I was told.'

'And who told you?'

'It was an old Welsh schoolmaster—Llewelyn Price, from Morvedd.'

'Well, I'll blowed! Shades of the misty, murky past!'

She rose to her feet.

'And who especially did you want? I suppose it's got got to be Rosemary because you see, *I'm* Sylvia!'

She held out her hand.

'*Sylvia?*'

It was more than Rachel could believe.

'It's a fact. Sylvia Ward, that was. Married a penniless houseman and now look at me! Mistress of the house where once I existed on baked beans and jam butties! I'm Sylvia Carson, now!'

Rachel tried to smile when all the time she felt like weeping great tears of joy. It simply couldn't be true. She had come almost in dread, wondering what fresh disappointment she would have to face, yet here she was, talking to Sylvia, Rosemary's friend.

'Oh, I don't believe it!' she gasped. 'I just can't believe it! I expected to come up against a brick wall again and here one of you is!'

'Well, if you'd come a year ago, you'd not have found me. We have only just moved in. My husband and I were looking for a town house and this one was advertised for sale. It needed a lot of work, but it's been worth it. Of course, we use it all, now. No more bedsits,' she smiled.

'Then this is my lucky day. You see, it's very important that I find Rosemary.'

'Well, it's a long time since Rosie and me lived here...'

Rachel detected a note of caution, now, in Sylvia Carson's voice. But that was only to be expected, she reasoned. Mrs Carson wasn't going to give out information to any stranger who came calling, was she? Not at least until she knew the enquiry was genuine? There was only one thing to do, Rachel decided, and that was to tell the whole truth. Sylvia had been Rosemary's friend—surely she would understand.

She said,

'Forgive me, Mrs Carson, but—'

'Sylvia. Do call me Sylvia. After all, we're most likely old bed-pan buddies, for all I know,' she smiled.

'Thanks. We're not, though. I wasn't a nurse, but please call me Rachel? And will you believe that what I'm going to ask you is not prompted by idle curiosity? I ask it with the best of intentions. Look, are you sure I'm not interrupting anything—taking up your time?'

'Quite sure. My husband won't be home until late. To tell you the truth, I'd be glad of your company.'

'Then I'll tell you why I'm looking for Rosemary. It really concerns Anne, my daughter—my adopted daughter. I think Rosemary was her mother, you see. But you'd know about the baby, I suppose. Anne is nearly nineteen and Rosemary lived here about twenty years ago according to Mr Price, so it fits, doesn't it? She would tell you, wouldn't she?'

For a moment there was an uneasy silence then Sylvia Carson said,

'Rosemary had a baby? Is that what you're trying to say?'

'Yes. I'm almost sure that the Rosemary Jones who lived here had a little girl in the Mother and Baby Home in Manchester. Do you mean you didn't know?'

'No, I didn't,' Sylvia returned soberly. 'I didn't know at all.'

'But you lived together, you worked together,' Rachel gasped. 'Surely you'd know—or suspect?'

The gnawing was back in Rachel's stomach, her throat suddenly choked with apprehension.

'We shared a bed-sitter and kitchen, but we worked different shifts. We didn't see all that much of each other. It was deliberately done, you see. When Rosemary was on nights she slept in the day and vice-versa with me. It worked out well that way; we weren't living in each other's pockets. Sort of Box and Cox, you could have called us. When one was out, the other was in. We met on days off, of course, and briefly, sometimes at shift changes.'

She shrugged and smiled.

'It also meant that neither of us had to make herself scarce when boy-friends called, if you see what I mean.'

'Yes,' Rachel whispered, staring fixedly at the dregs in her tea-cup. 'But didn't you know anything about her? Who was her boy-friend, for instance? Surely you met him?'

'I didn't and that's a fact. He probably lived in Yorkshire. You know her sister lived there, I suppose?'

'Yes, but Mr Price didn't know where. It was Rosemary he kept in touch with. They wrote to each other for about two years, he said, then the letters suddenly stopped. His own were sent back to him, marked "Gone Away".'

'Yes—it was most likely me who returned them.'

'And Rosemary just left? Without giving you an address? Without even telling you about the baby?'

'Yes—but then she wouldn't tell me, would she? I mean, if she'd got pregnant, it's not likely she would shout it around. You didn't in those days, you know.'

'Yes,' Rachel nodded. Then with one last despairing effort she said,

'You can't remember Rosemary ever mentioning where her sister lived, can you?'

'No Rachel, I can't. But they were fairly close, I know that. Whenever she had time off, Rosemary always went to Yorkshire to see Mair—even if it was only for a few hours. Perhaps that's where you should look for—'

She hesitated.

'For the father of her child?' Rachel supplied, quietly.

Sylvia Carson nodded.

'I think if you're going to get a lead, it'll be in Yorkshire. Like I said, Rosie went there a lot. We didn't get much in the way of wages in our probationer days, but that didn't stop her. Most times she hitched a lift. I didn't hold with hitching; I said so, but she took no notice. That's what makes me think the man in her life lived there, because in my young days, respectable girls didn't hitch lifts, either. That guy must have been something special to make her do that. You see, normally she was such a quiet little mouse. Not like me. I was the wild one—not Rosemary.'

'So I've come to a dead end again,' Rachel whispered bitterly. 'I'm not muck-raking, believe me. It really is important that I find Rosemary. Our family doctor agrees with me, too. It's affecting Anne, you see. A few years back some wretched girl at school said her mother must have been a tart and the trouble it's led to—'

'A tart? Rosemary Jones a tart? Well, that's a laugh. She was the nicest, sweetest girl you could wish for and she would have made a fine nurse, too, if she'd had the sense to go on with her training.'

'The hospital!' Rachel gasped. 'I'd almost forgotten. Which hospital did you both train at? Maybe there would be old records that would help?'

'I doubt it very much. The hospital Rosemary and I worked at was old—it was demolished fifteen years ago when the big new place was built. I doubt they'd have personnel records now. I'm sure of it, in fact. But look,' she hastened, 'leave me your address and phone number. I'll see if my husband can help at all. If he can, I could get in touch.'

'You would? Oh, I'd be so grateful. Phone *me* if you ever have any news, would you? You see,' she hesitated, wanting to be wholly truthful, 'my husband doesn't know what I am doing. John doesn't think it's a good idea, at all. If your husband has any ethical scruples, I'll give you the name of our own doctor—Bill Lee will bear me out, I promise you.'

Rachel wrote the addresses on a page torn from her diary and handed them to Sylvia Carson.

'Somehow I knew I'd not have any luck here, either,' she whispered despondently, 'but if you can help, if you can remember any little thing, I would be so grateful, Mrs Carson. And I really would respect Rosemary's privacy. Please believe me, it means so much to Anne to meet her other mother—to see Rosemary.'

'Yes, I can well understand. She's at an age to feel everything intensely—joy or sorrow. But I think you'll have to prepare her—and yourself, Rachel—to accept that you might never find Rosemary. Had you thought she might even be living at the other end of the world?'

Sylvia Carson smiled gently.

'Why don't you just tell your daughter that Rosemary was a very sweet girl—you can take my word for that. And if you like, I'll give you something for Anne. There's a photo of Rosemary and I, taken on holiday. If your daughter saw it, it might help to convince her.'

'Oh, how good of you—I'd love to have it, if you're sure?'

'Sure I'm sure—I know just where to find it. Won't take a minute.'

So that was all there was to be, Rachel thought sadly. That was what Anne would have to content herself with for the present—a photograph and assurances. But it wasn't going to be enough, Rachel realized, panic rising in her throat. Anne was determined to meet her other mother, to see for herself what she was like. Nothing less would suffice because to that end Anne had already got herself into trouble with the police and broken off her engagement.

Why, oh why did I start it all? Rachel fretted. What made me make that stupid promise to Anne and raise her hopes so? Where is it all going to end?

'Here we are then,' Sylvia Carson said brightly. 'Taken near the top of Snowdon—the summer before—' she hesitated, '—before Rosemary went away.'

Rachel gave a gasp of disbelief. There was no mistaking Rosemary Jones, for there, too, was Anne; the same delicate colouring, the deep blue eyes, the long, cornsilk hair and the hesitant half-smile.

Tears rushed to Rachel's eyes as she fumbled in her handbag for her notecase.

'Look,' she whispered. 'See what I mean?'

She held out a photograph of Anne.

'Now you know I'm telling you the truth. That's Anne, taken last year. She couldn't be anyone else's daughter but Rosemary's, could she?'

Slowly the other woman nodded her head.

'Rosemary's girl,' she whispered, 'and she's grown into a beauty.'

Then she held out her hand as Rachel gathered up her scarf and gloves.

'I do sympathize with you, my dear, but you'll have to accept that you have set yourself a near-impossible task.'

'I know that,' Rachel whispered, slipping the precious photograph into her handbag, 'but thank you for being so kind to me. I suppose now I've got to try the long, hard way—letters to papers, the Salvation Army, Social Security records...'

Sylvia Carson waved good-bye to the dejected figure who turned briefly at the gate then closed the door quietly.

Damn! Damn! Damn! she jerked. After all these years, why on earth did people want to start raking up the past? It was all over and done with, wasn't it?

She looked at the folded paper between her fingers. Best destroy it, she thought. Best she shouldn't know where Rachel lived. She had felt a bit of a stinker, lying as she had done, but after nearly twenty years—well, it just wasn't fair, she reasoned.

But for all that, she found herself reading the names and addresses written there—maybe just in case?—before she tore up the paper, and as she did so, her mouth went suddenly dry.

'No!' she whispered, her fingers tingling to their very tips with apprehension. 'No! *It can't be!*'

Reaching blindly for the telephone that stood beside her on the hall table, she dialled a number. She wanted there to be no reply to her call. She didn't want to do what she was doing. She should have more sense, she knew it. Sleeping dogs, and all that. But Rachel Parker wasn't going to be all that easily put off. She wasn't the type to let it drop.

The telephone continued to ring. There was no reply, Sylvia Carson decided with relief and maybe it was as well. Perhaps it would be better to wait and talk things over husband when he got home.

Exactly as she decided to hang up, the ringing ceased abruptly.

'Hullo? 78418...?'

Too late! She took a deep breath then said,

'Hi there! Syl. here. You alone? I mean, can you talk? Well, listen then. Someone's just been here. She was looking for Rosemary Jones, she said. Told me she had every reason to believe that Rosemary was from Morvedd and that she'd had a baby in Manchester—a little girl who was adopted...'

There was a small, strained silence then she went on impatiently,

'Yes, I know that and believe me she got nothing out of me that would help her, but do you know who that woman was? She left her name and address with me and it's only just struck me. She was called Rachel Parker. Yes, that's what I said. *Parker*. And what's more, her husband's name was *John!*'

Disconsolately Rachel shivered in the queue outside the station telephone kiosks. The morning that began so brightly, so hopefully, had suddenly and perversely turned into a near-winter's day. A cold rampaging wind blew gusts into her face and her feet were very cold. The nearer she had travelled towards Birmingham, the worse the weather had become, matching itself to her misery, the rain splashes on the compartment window like the tears she longed to shed.

The strongest, the most water-tight security wall there is.

That was what Dan had said she was up against. He had warned her but she had been so sure she was right, so certain she would find Rosemary and all would be well again with Anne's world.

A man nodded as he held open the kiosk door and Rachel managed a small smile, glad to be out of the cold, the noise of the station. She dialled Steele's office number, a coin at the ready in her hand, but there was no reply. The fingers on the large clock outside pointed to 5.50. Dan would have gone home now, wouldn't he? The Courts would have finished their business for the day. Commonsense told her to return to Fair Oaks, to ring Anne and ask her to come home; to admit, no matter how it might hurt, that she had found nothing. Admit, too, that she had been wrong ever to suggest they should look for Rosemary.

But a photograph wouldn't be enough for Anne.

There was a streak of stubbornness in her that didn't take any kind of defeat easily. It seemed that there was nothing for it but to go along to Dan Steele's flat. At least if she did that, she could postpone facing Anne for a little while longer and Dan had said to do that, hadn't he—to let him know how she had got on in Manchester? And perhaps he could tell her if there was anything more she could do. There was so little time left. Soon John would be back.

She clucked impatiently. John could be so unreasonable, she sighed. If only he would try to understand, help her a little. Why did he have to be so dogmatic, so utterly insensitive to Anne's needs?

So commonsense did not prevail; Rachel did not return to Fair Oaks, because Daniel Steele was just a few minutes walk away and John was in Rotterdam; because John didn't care, Rachel thought rebelliously and Dan did and she was so desperately in need of comfort ...

EIGHT

She had known he would be there to answer her knock —Fate couldn't have dealt her another body-blow—and she had known he would say,

'Hullo, Rachel,' very softly as if to tell her he had been waiting for her. It seemed right that he should take her hand and lead her into the warm firelight, sitting her on the settee, saying gently,

'You're cold. Your hands are like ice.'

Tenderly he removed her wet shoes and rubbed her feet with his big, awkward hands.

'No luck, then?'

'No, Dan.'

'Here, you need a drink. What'll it be? Scotch? Brandy?'

'Nothing, thanks. Just a cup of tea, if it's not too much trouble.'

He said it wasn't, that she was just to sit there and get warm.

'I'm in Court again tomorrow,' he called regretfully from the kitchen, wanting to get the bad news over with.

'That figures,' Rachel whispered numbly, staring into the leaping flames.

The room was not what she had expected to find. It was neat—but then she knew he had been expecting her—and the furniture was good, the loose covers on the settee and deep armchairs bright and well-fitting.

Steele pulled out a small table and set tea cups on it. They were of fragile gold-edged china in the palest green. He had probably got them out especially for her and she wished he hadn't. They had been Elaine's cups, she knew it, and it had been Elaine who once chose the material for the covers and the prints that hung in clusters on the walls. All this had been part of Dan Steele's marriage before it was split with legal precision into equal parts marked His and Hers.

A stab of pain ran through Rachel, and it surprised her that such a thing could have the power to hurt her. It was a long time before she spoke and when she did, the words came in sad little whispers.

'It wasn't any good, Dan. I've seen Sylvia—yes, she was actually there at the address Mr Price gave us.'

Haltingly she told him all that had happened, leaving nothing out, turning the knife that jabbed into her with every despairing word. And as if pain and despair were not enough, she took out the photographs, Rosemary's and Anne's and held them side by side.

'There's no denying it. There's no doubt that Rosemary Jones from Morvedd is Anne's mother, but where is she? I'm so muddled, so unhappy ...'

Her plea ended in a whispered sob and she covered her face with hands that trembled.

Unspeaking, Steele reached out, taking her hands, holding them firmly in his. Then gently he drew her to him, stroking her hair, whispering softly,

'All right, Rachel—let it come. Don't bottle it up.'

She knew it was wrong. She had no right to go to him so eagerly, so hungrily. She pulled away from him a little, looking up into his face and he bent down and touched her lips gently with his own, stilling her protest, making little sounds of comfort.

'Dan,' Rachel choked. 'We mustn't.'

But he kissed her eyelids and the tip of her nose and the tears that slipped down her cheeks. Then suddenly his lips were seeking hers, gently at first then fiercely as he felt her body soft against his.

'Don't go? Stay with me?' he pleaded. 'I need you, Rachel. I need you so much!'

His voice was urgent and demanding. There was no denying its meaning and the whole of her body throbbed with a savage answering need. She closed her eyes as he kissed the hollow in her throat and her body ached for the touch of his hands. It was so wrong and so right. She felt afraid and ecstatic. She didn't care. Later, perhaps, but not now.

Gently he cupped her breasts in his hands.

'Rachel. Rachel, sweetheart...'

Inside her the coiled spring snapped and her body became limp and yielding.

'Dan,' she whispered, her mouth searching for his.

He did not speak. Instead he kissed away the tears that clung to her lashes, teasing her with his lips, urging her to match his passion with her own and she responded gladly. She heard his groan that was part despair part triumph and she took his face between her hands and looked into his eyes.

'Yes, darling. Oh, please, yes!' she exulted.

Only for a moment did disbelief flicker in his eyes then he gathered her into his arms, lifting her easily. She laid her head on his chest and relaxed against him.

'Rachel,' he choked. 'Oh, Rachel, love.'

She felt his heart bumping madly as her own and

she touched the tip of his chin with her lips. His face was soft as if he had newly shaved.

'You're sure?' he demanded roughly, pushing open the bedroom door. 'You're very sure, darling?'

'Yes,' she whispered. 'Very sure.'

They lay together afterwards, their bodies warm, neither of them wanting to speak or to part, wondering at the fierceness of their loving, unwilling to break the spell.

This is not me, she thought. The woman so safe in Dan Steele's arms is not Rachel Parker. Rachel would not do as I have done. Who is this strange, wanton creature? Have I only just come alive? Did I die a little after the Manchester-time? Have I been waiting all my life for this awakening?

'Rachel?'

Dan stirred, shifting his arm, tilting her face to his, kissing her gently, without passion.

'All right, darling?'

His voice was anxious.

'Yes, Dan.'

'No regrets?'

She shook her head. She had none—not now, at least. Later? She didn't know about later.

'Did you know it would happen—when you came here tonight? Did you want me as much as I wanted you, Rachel?'

'I think I did, only I didn't know it. I think I have needed you for a long time.'

He didn't say, 'What do we do now?' and she was glad because she was still that strange wanton and that made it all right. Soon she would have to leave him, dress herself in Rachel's Parker's clothes, assume Rachel's identity once more. But until then, she didn't want to talk about it.

Give me just a little more time, she yearned silently, knowing inside her that that was all she could ask, wondering how she would tell him.

How would she tell him? Would she demand to know what they had been thinking about? Would she look into his dear face and see her own bewilderment mirrored in his eyes?

She looked at her watch.

'It's nearly nine o'clock,' she whispered.

'Stay?' he pleaded. 'There's nothing for you to go home to.'

'No, Dan.'

Rachel was speaking now. She with her sense of motherly duty was taking over and making it easier.

'I must go. I promised Anne I would phone her, let her know how I got on.'

'No, darling. Don't go. If you do, I shall never see you again.'

'You will, Dan. I promise you will, but take me home now—*please?*'

'You really want me to?'

'Dan, I shouldn't be here at all.'

Evading his question she dropped her eyes, unable to continue. She knew it should end between them and end at once, before it gathered such momentum that it spun and slid giddily out of their control. She knew it, but she was uncertain, still.

'Take me back. Let me get my bearings—think things out?'

'All right,' he agreed reluctantly, 'but promise me

you won't lie awake half the night, worrying about it?'

'I won't.'

Yet for all her assurances, she sat unspeaking by his side as he drove her towards Fair Oaks. Shocked and bemused, she tried to get the whole thing into proportion.

What had happened, she pondered and why had it happened? She had let John down and Anne and herself. But she had needed so desperately to be loved and to give love and she could only feel regret that it ought to end. There was no shame in her heart. It had been good between them. She had been sickened by all the material things around her and saddened by a husband who had turned into a man so preoccupied with riches that he had no time to spare for her or for Anne. So often, lately, Rachel had found herself wishing they could be back in that first little house, with John coming home to her, eager to share his troubles and triumphs and his heart—oh, most of all, his heart. But the Manchester-time was long gone, and with it something precious. Who then could blame her? Had she been so wrong to seek comfort? Did one act of loving make her into a wanton, a tart?

She shivered. They had called Rosemary a tart, hadn't they?

A sudden changing of gears jerked away her muddled thoughts. They were stationary now, waiting the passing of an oncoming car before turning into the drive at Fair Oaks, that desirable property she called home. As they drove into the wide path, Rachel's eyes opened wide and she gave a gasp of alarm.

'Someone's there!'

A light shone from the landing window and the garage doors were open wide. Steele jammed on the brake.

'Wait here,' he said, 'I'll take a look. You expecting anybody?'

'No. Be careful, Dan?'

He tweaked her nose gently and smiled.

'Sure. Sure.'

He was back almost at once.

'There's a red Mini outside,' he said. 'Is it yours?'

He repeated the registration number.

'Yes,' Rachel let out a sigh of relief. 'Anne must be back.'

'Shall I come in with you—just to be sure?'

'No thanks, Dan. Best that you shouldn't.'

Suddenly Rachel felt vaguely apprehensive.

'I'll phone you tomorrow, Rachel—before I go into Court.'

'Yes please. Do that.'

She didn't quite know what to say or how to take her leave of him.

'Well, Dan ... ?'

She looked up into his eyes. He didn't try to touch her. He just said,

'I love you, Rachel,' then turned abruptly and walked towards his car.

Anne was standing in the doorway as Rachel walked slowly up the steps.

'It's you Anne—you're home?'

It was a silly thing to say, Rachel thought, but you didn't talk sense when your whole world had turned upside down and landed in a heart-tearing muddle at your feet. Touching her burning cheeks she wondered if what had happened showed on her face.

'Mum! Thank goodness you're back! You'd better get on the phone to Aunt Joyce straight away. I've told him you're out with her!'

Rachel stared blankly into Anne's agitated face.

'Who? Told *who*?'

'Dad, of course. He was here when I arrived. He's back. Mum. Dad's back!'

'But he said Friday,' Rachel gasped.

'Well, he was here when I got home, so you'd better do something quick, unless you want him to know what you've been doing. And he doesn't know, does he?'

'No, he doesn't,' Rachel whispered, dry-mouthed. 'Where is he now?'

'He went to the office for something. You'd better hurry; he said he wouldn't be long.'

That's it, Rachel thought wildly, hurry and involve your best friend. Cover your tracks so your husband won't know you've been looking for Anne's mother against his wishes; so he won't find out that less than an hour ago you were in Dan Steele's arms.

A brooding sense of unease washed over Rachel but did she really have a choice, she asked herself as she lifted the phone.

'Hi, Joyce. Be a pal and do me a favour?'

She felt shocked that her voice could sound so normal.

'John's home and I've been to Manchester. I need an alibi—just this once? I won't ask you again.'

'That's O.K. love. All in a good cause. Did you have any luck, by the way?'

'Not really.'

Briefly Rachel recounted the day's happenings.

'I seem to have come to another dead end,' she finished.

'I don't know where to go from here.'

'You'll think of something. Look, Rachel, we'll talk about it tomorrow. Bill's on call tonight and I daren't hog the line.'

When Rachel put down the phone, Anne was standing eagerly at her side.

'What was that you said to Aunt Joyce? You've got a photograph of Rosemary? Oh, let me see it?'

Glad to be able to offer some small comfort, Rachel handed over the snapshot.

'It's all I've been able to manage, Anne. At first I thought I was really on to something. I couldn't believe it when Rosemary's friend was still living in the house. But she couldn't tell me anything. She didn't even know about you. Rosemary just vanished, she said.'

But Anne heard nothing of what Rachel was saying. Her face trembled between laughter and tears as she whispered,

'It's really her—my other mother? She looks such a sweet person.'

'I *know* she was, Anne. Rosemary Jones wasn't a tart. If you never meet her, at least you can be sure of that,' Rachel urged.

'But I *must* see her now! For years I misjudged her and I've got to put things right—tell her how glad I am she had me.'

'But Anne, couldn't you be content to know that everyone I spoke to liked her?' Rachel whispered.

The front door slammed.

'Dad!'

Hastily Anne pushed Rosemary's picture into the pocket of her skirt as John flung into the room, his face flushed with anger.

'So you're back, Rachel? Where have you been?'

'At Joyce's.'

'I don't believe you! You've been looking for Anne's mother when you gave me your word you wouldn't!'

'I didn't give my word, John.'

'All right, but you led me to believe you would forget the whole thing.'

'Then you misunderstood, and I'm sorry.'

There was no need to ask how he knew, Rachel thought bitterly. He had read the phone message from Mr Whitaker. It would have been waiting there for him on his desk. What a fool she had been to forget it. Why hadn't she told Anne to destroy it?

'You've been on to Mr Whitaker,' she accused, hotly. 'He's as nice as pie to my face, but the moment my back is turned, he sneaks to you!'

'No Rachel—he just felt I should know. He didn't agree with what you are doing.'

'It was nothing to do with him!' Rachel flamed.

'But you involved him, so it was!'

John's face was stiff with rage and Rachel began to tremble. She had never before seen her husband give way to such white-hot anger. She swallowed noisily. It hurt her throat and she couldn't speak. Suddenly, her whole world seemed to shatter. Could it have been so short a time ago that she was with Dan, safe and loved and wanted? And they had loved. Until now it had seemed right and good, but John's presence changed everything. She wondered if it showed on her face, in her eyes. Suddenly she felt cheap and nasty.

'This business has got to stop!' John's voice ripped into her thoughts. 'Do you understand me, Rachel! I will not have it!'

Rachel flinched. For one fear-filled moment she thought he would strike her.

'*Do you understand?*' he ground.

Stung to anger, Rachel found her voice.

'How dare you tell me what to do? How *dare* you?' she choked.

In an instant, Anne was by her side.

'Stop it, Dad! Stop it, both of you. I won't listen to any more!'

Head down, tears shining in her eyes, Anne flung from the room. Stunned, they heard her feet pounding the stairs and the slam of a bedroom door. A sudden silence hung on the air as each faced the other in unspoken accusation, then with deliberate quiet Rachel said,

'I'm sorry if you misunderstood my motive, John. I thought Anne would be happy if I found Rosemary.'

'Rosemary! *You know her name?* Just what have you found out, Rachel? Who have you been talking to?'

John's face was drained of colour, his lips stiff with disbelief.

'Well, I got nowhere with Mr Whitaker, so I went to an Inquiry Agent,' Rachel tossed her head defiantly. 'He soon found out that Anne's mother was called Rosemary Jones and that once she lived in North Wales. But that's all,' she countered, deliberately ignoring her visit to Sylvia Carson's, 'except that Rosemary has a sister called Mair who went to Yorkshire to live. I know nothing more. In fact,' she shrugged, 'you'll be glad to know I've come to a dead end.'

'Not glad, Rachel, just plain thankful, although how you could have been so utterly stupid is beyond me. And to go to the lengths of hiring a private eye—'

Rachel tilted her head and gazed silently into her husband's eyes. She wanted to hurl the full force of her resentment at him but for Anne's sake she dare not risk another quarrel. It was as if, she thought, they were drifting steadily back to the misery of the time in Manchester when she knew for certain she could never have a child of her own. There had been a long bitterness between them then and she had silently hugged her unhappiness to her aching, barren body and prayed for the miracle it needed to save their marriage.

Anne had been that miracle but there would be no second chances. They were growing apart again and suddenly Rachel was too weary to care. With a sadness that tore through her like a pain, she realized she had reached the limit of her endurance. She rose to her feet and walked slowly across the room. At the door she turned and said,

'I'm going to bed. I have a headache.'

'That's fine by me,' John jerked. 'I won't disturb you. I'll sleep in the spare room!'

Abruptly he turned away from her and opened his brief-case.

The ringing above Rachel's head drew nearer, grew louder, then settled level with her ear, each purr vibrating in her aching head like a hammer-blow.

'Uh?'

She reached out and grasped the telephone.

'Rachel?'

'Hm. John?'

Why was he calling at this unearthly hour? She remembered then that he was no longer in Rotterdam, that last night he had slept in the spare room, that she and Dan ...

'Rachel, it's nearly half-past eleven.'

'*What?*'

She sat bolt upright in bed, wincing as the hammers inside her head banged harder.

'I left early this morning, Rachel. I was at work before seven. I tried not to disturb you ...'

'I must have slept through the alarm,' she replied.

But she could hardly be blamed for that, she thought petulantly, since she had lain awake, unhappy and wide-eyed, until almost daybreak.

'Do you want something, John, or did you call to tell me what the time is?'

'Look Rachel, I'm sorry if I wakened you. It's just that Anne isn't at **work**.'

'Oh, heavens!'

She had let Anne oversleep, too.

'I'll get her up,' she said stiffly, knowing how John disliked lateness, realizing that although Anne worked for her father's firm, she was allowed no favours.

'You can always stop her half a day's pay,' she retorted childishly, subconsciously picking up the threads of their unfinished quarrel.

'Rachel, I'm sorry about last night. I shouldn't have lost my temper, especially in front of Anne.'

Rachel drew in an indignant breath. She knew she should try to meet John half way, but she could not.

'I brought some perfume back for you, Rachel. I left it on the dressing-table.'

'How nice. Thank you very much.'

Her thanks were stiff and insincere.

'I'll try not to be too late home tonight ...'

'Yes. All right.'

Rachel slammed down the receiver then immediately regretted it. Worried, tired, her head aching miserably, she threw back the bed-clothes. She was behaving stupidly and it was all because she felt guilty about Dan Steele and was trying to throw that guilt back on John. Shrugging into her housecoat, she padded barefoot along the landing to Anne's room.

'Hey there, lazy—'

Rachel's sleep-heavy eyes jerked wide open. The bed was made, the room tidy and empty and fear iced its way down her back as she looked at the dressing-table and saw the envelope.

'Oh, please—no!'

She knew the worst before her trembling fingers had ripped it open. The note was pathetic and short.

Dear Mum and Dad,
  I seem to cause nothing but trouble between you. Please forgive me? I've got to straighten myself out. I love you both very much.
                              Anne.

NINE

'Oh, no!' Rachel whispered to the empty, echoing room. 'Oh, Anne...'

When did she go? Where was she now? What was she doing?

Panic seized her limbs, shaking them violently. Blindly she ran back to the bedroom and picked up the phone. Sick with fear she dialled Parker's Haulage.

'I can't get hold of him at the moment, Mrs Parker, but I'll get him to call you back,' Miss Tremlitt's safe, sane voice assured her.

Rachel reached for a cigarette. Normally she did not smoke and it made her feel slightly sick. Fascinated, she watched the smoke curl upwards in little jerky spirals as her hand trembled uncontrollably. At the first purr she snatched up the phone. John said,

'Rachel, what is it? What's so important that—'

'Anne's gone! She wasn't in her room. She left a note saying she was sorry and that she had to sort herself out!'

'But *where* has she gone?'

'Oh, how do I know? Do you think I'd have phoned you if I did?'

'No, Rachel,' came the curt reply, 'not for a minute.'

'Well, can you come home? Shall I ring the police?'

'No, I can't come home. I'm much too busy. And if you call the police, they'll tell you it's a domestic matter and they can't interfere. Anne's an adult, now.'

'But she might do something!'

'And she might *not*. She's having a tantrum, Rachel. She'll be back. Anyway, I've had enough of police stations for a while, thanks all the same!'

'Anne is desperate,' Rachel pleaded. 'I know it from her letter.'

'No—I think she's upset, maybe, but that's nothing new these days.' John sighed wearily, 'Give her a chance to calm down. She'll be back, there's nothing so sure. Just try not to worry—all right?'

Rachel heard the click of a replaced receiver and the impersonal purring of a dead line.

He really doesn't care, she thought. Anne has run away and all he can think about is Parker's.

Slamming down the receiver, she shook her head with disbelief.

'I could almost hate you,' she whispered passionately, '... *hate* you, John Parker!'

Tears pricked her eyes and choked her throat but she refused to give way to them. Anger was flaming white-hot inside her now and she had no time to waste in weeping. For one crazy moment she wanted to take something and hurl it to the floor with all her strength but instead she filled her lungs with great gulps of air like a spent runner.

Calmer, she flopped on to the bed. Of course she couldn't go to the police—not so soon after the shoplifting incident. Oh, why was Dan in Court? He had promised to ring her. Most probably he had done so and she had slept through his call, she realized.

Should she phone Joyce, then, or Maggie Dean? Was Anne only having a tantrum or was there something more to it—something far more sinister?

Distantly the door bell rang. With a cry of hope Rachel ran downstairs. Anne? She was back?

It was Graham Hobson who stood on the doorstep.

'Hullo, Mrs Parker. Look—I don't want to bother you, but I was driving through town not long ago and I saw Anne. She didn't look very well, so when I got back to the office, I phoned her at Parker's Haulage. They told me she hadn't been in to work.'

'Graham! Thank heaven you came,' Rachel gulped with relief, motioning to him to come inside. 'Anne's gone—she left a note that I can't make head or tail of. Where did you see her?'

'In the city centre. By the time I was able to stop the car, she was gone. She looked dazed.'

'That figures. Oh, Graham, I'm so worried that I'm just about ready to blow my top.'

'What does Mr Parker think?'

'Mr Parker is busy!'

Rachel could not disguise the bitterness in her voice.

'He says it's a storm in a teacup, or words to that effect. What he really means is that Parker's need him more than Anne and I do.'

There was a small, embarrassed pause then Graham said,

'What say I nip back into town and have a look for Anne? There are one or two places I think she could be.'

'Oh, would you Graham, and could I come too? I can't stay here, just doing nothing. I wouldn't be long, getting dressed.

'Sure,' he smiled, 'and I'll fix us a coffee, uh, while I'm waiting?'

'Bless you,' Rachel whispered.

Oh, what a blind little fool Anne was to treat him so badly.

Rachel looked down at her bare feet. She must pull herself together. Every instinct told her that time was precious.

'Just give me a couple of minutes?' she said.

Graham parked the car then fed a coin into the meter. He didn't know why, but all his instincts urged him to Kirby and Ward's. Anne had been near there when first he saw her, walking aimlessly, her eyes downcast. Asked to explain himself, he thought, he could not have done so, for who would want to return to a department store where only two weeks ago they had been caught shop-lifting? But the look he had seen on Anne's face troubled him and he knew that right now she might well do something quite inexplicable. Taking Rachel's arm he said gently,

'I don't want to worry you, but I think we should go to Kirby and Ward's.

He heard the sharp intake of Rachel's breath, saw fear flash briefly in her eyes but she whispered,

'All right. What ever you think.'

Soon, she feared, the store would be crowded with lunchtime shoppers and finding anyone in such a place would be near impossible.

'Did you notice what Anne was wearing this morning, Graham?'

'Yes, the blue denim suit, I think. And she had a red scarf with it. Anne's tall. She would be fairly easy to spot, if she's in there.'

'Where shall we start?'

'Best we separate, I think. You take the escalator, Mrs Parker. Go all the way up then down again. You should get a fair view of each floor that way. I'll take the stairs and we'll meet down here again as soon as we're through. Okay?'

Rachel nodded.

'Do you really think she's here, Graham?'

'Maybe not,' he replied cautiously, forcing a smile of comfort, 'but it's best to be sure.'

Rachel was waiting at the foot of the escalator when Graham strode towards her. He had had no luck, but the look in Rachel's eyes caused his muscles to tense. She walked quickly to meet him. Grasping his arm she said,

'Look—over there—that man with the green carrier-bag. I know him. I'm sure of it!'

The face ran alarm-bells in Graham's brain. The man was wearing a hat now and his clothes were different, but somewhere, not so long ago, Graham too had seen him. It hit him in a flash. The Court, when Anne had been charged. He was the man who had given evidence for Kirby and Ward.

'I know him too,' he gasped. 'He's the store detective. He's watching someone.'

Together they walked nearer.

The man's eyes were fixed steadily in the direction of the costume jewellery counter where a girl stood unmoving. She was tall and fair-haired. She was wearing denims and a bright red scarf.

Rachel called, 'Anne!'

'No, Mrs Parker. Leave this to me. Stay here!'

Something in Graham's voice stopped Rachel and

she knew he was right. Suddenly she felt drained by fear, incapable of thinking clearly, of acting positively. She nodded her head.

'Be careful?' she pleaded, huskily.

'Anne,' Graham whispered and in a moment he was by her side. 'Darling. What are you doing here,' he asked. 'What's wrong?'

She didn't turn her head or give any indication that she had even heard him. She was staring with hypnotic gaze at a display of cheap, heart-shaped turquoise pendants.

'Anne,' Graham hissed, taking her arm roughly, forcing her to look at him, breaking the trance. 'What are you trying to do?'

Her blue eyes opened wide. As if seeing him for the first time she said wonderingly,

'Graham? Graham, it's you...'

He pulled her away from the tantalizing lockets.

'Anne—I'm sorry, but I've got to ask this. Have you taken anything? The store detective is over there and if you've got anything on you that you haven't paid for, he'll follow you and arrest you as soon as you walk out of the place. You realize that, don't you?'

'Got anything? N—no—I don't think so...'

'Turn out your pockets,' Graham insisted grimly. 'Go on, Anne. Do as I say!'

Obediently, she did as he demanded. There was nothing in them that should not have been there and he sighed with relief.

'Sorry, but I had to be sure. Now, I'm taking you home and I don't want any scenes. All right?'

She nodded.

'Oh, Graham,' she whispered.

She held out her hand to him in a childlike, beseeching gesture and he entwined her fingers in his. Then tucking her arm beneath his own, he walked her firmly past the store detective to where Rachel waited.

'It's all right. It's all over now, darling,' he smiled.

Together, they walked into the street outside.

Attentively Graham settled Rachel and Anne in the back seat of his car, gently tucking a rug around Anne's trembling body.

'That better?'

'Yes, thanks—fine,' Rachel nodded, placing her arm around her daughter's shoulders, drawing her protectively towards her. She waited until Graham had edged into the main traffic stream then said quietly,

'Want to talk about it, Anne?'

If only she would, Rachel thought, it might help rid her of the confusion that seemed to have plagued her for so long. Loving Anne as she did, she wanted to help, yet felt so desperately inadequate.

'Oh, Mum,' Anne whispered forlornly, 'I've made such a mess of things. I'm a selfish, spoiled brat and I shouldn't have wanted to find my other mother. I never imagined it would be so difficult or cause so much trouble—like last night, I mean. I've never seen Dad in such a rage. I was terrified . . .'

She stared ahead, wide-eyed at the memory of it, struggling hard to control her emotions.

'Now you're both at each other's throats,' she whispered. 'I know Dad slept in the spare room last night and it's my fault. I'm a rotten little cat. You should have left me at that Home. Oh, if only I could make myself forget Rosemary!'

Tears began to fall then, hot and bitter.

'There now,' Rachel soothed, as if the years had rolled away and Anne was a little girl again. 'It'll all come right,' she whispered tenderly. 'Don't bottle it up any longer.'

She held Anne tightly until the storm inside her had passed and her body lay limp and spent.

'That better?'

Anne nodded and taking the tissue Rachel offered said jerkily,

'I was going to take another locket, you realize that, don't you, Mum? I didn't care. I just wanted to hit out at somebody.'

'But you didn't take one, so it doesn't matter.'

'No. I just stood there and thought what a stupid little fool I was and how I'd best start growing up, pretty quick. Suddenly I loved you and Dad so much that it hurt.'

Rachel dropped a kiss on the top of Anne's head.

'That was a pretty nice thing to say,' she whispered huskily.

In the driving mirror she met Graham's eyes and gave him a little smile. He grinned back and nodded his head, a comforting little gesture that told her not to worry.

They sat in silence for the rest of the drive home, all of them seemingly deep in thought, then for the first time, Graham spoke.

'Looks like your father's home, Anne.'

Anne nodded, staring ahead blankly at the car parked by the front door.

'Reckon he is at that. I think you'd better not stay,

Graham,' she whispered, 'unless you want to bear witness to another bust-up!'

'There won't be any trouble,' Rachel said quietly, more confidently than she felt, 'and anyway, I want Graham to come in.'

As they opened the living-room door, John jumped angrily to his feet.

'Just where do you think you've been, Anne?' he exploded then bit on his anger as Graham silently shook his head in warning.

'Dad—I'm sorry. I'm truly sorry.'

She began to cry softly.

'Please don't be angry? Don't start yelling at each other again—not because of me?'

'I think she's just about all-in,' Graham interposed, looking levelly at John. 'Don't you think she would be better in bed, Mrs Parker?'

Rachel nodded, grateful for his wisdom.

'All right, Anne,' she whispered, 'nobody is going to get upset. Come on—let's get you into bed.'

When Rachel came downstairs again, John and Graham were sitting grim-faced and silent.

'I've given her hot milk and one of my tablets,' then smiling at Graham she said,

'I don't know what to say or how to begin to try to thank you. Goodness knows what Anne might have done if you hadn't—'

She broke off, confused.

'It's all right, Rachel,' John interrupted curtly, 'Graham has told me—*everything*. But how could Anne be so stupid—going back to that store again?'

'I don't know, John. I only know she is very unhappy

and whether her troubles are real or imagined, I can't help her any more. I can't take any more, either...'

She broke off, fighting emotion, determined not to break down before Graham. But Graham understood. This, he decided, was something Anne's parents would have to work out between themselves.

'Look,' he said, 'I'll have to get back to work now, but I'll look in later on, if that's all right?'

'Yes, Graham, I'd like that,' Rachel smiled as they walked together to the door.

John placed his hand to his throbbing head. He had taken, he decided, just about as much as he was able. Rachel's animosity was hard enough to bear; she, too, was just about at the end of her tether he knew, but Anne's uncompromising grief was the final straw. For so long he had tried and it had been far from easy. Now, it had to come to this, he thought with bitter resignation.

Rachel stood hesitantly in the doorway, feeling sharp unease as she saw her husband's closed eyes, his pinched, ashen face.

'All right, you win,' John said wearily.

'Win? What do you mean? There can't be a winner in this crazy game.'

'No, Rachel, there can't be, but I'm opting out anyway because I've had as much as I can take. I tried to warn you both and you wouldn't listen. O.K. If Anne still wants to meet her mother, she can.'

'You mean you don't mind any more? It's all right? You won't stop me trying to find Rosemary?' Rachel gasped.

'No, Rachel.'

Reluctantly John opened his eyes then tilted his head and squared his shoulders as if some unseen fist was about to deliver a blow to his jaw. Like a man suddenly grown old he rose to his feet and walked over to the sideboard. Pouring himself a drink he asked,

'Do you want one?'

'No thanks, John.'

For a moment they eyed each other warily then John said quietly,

'You don't have to look any more. I'll tell you where she is!'

'Rosemary? *You know* ...?'

Rachel's stomach contracted. Suddenly her heart began to thump.

'How do you know?' she insisted shrilly. 'Why did you let me go on looking? And why did you let Anne get so upset when all the time—'

'*Rachel!*'

John's voice was pitched low yet it sounded like the cracking of a whip.

She took a deep, shuddering breath and looked into his face. Her heart beat in her throat, loudly, urgently. Around them was a silence so ominous she could almost smell it. John whispered,

'Listen to me. For God's sake, *listen*! She's mine, Rachel. Anne is my daughter; *mine and Rosemary's!*'

Something akin to a physical blow seemed to crash into Rachel's face.

I am mad, she thought. There is a screaming in my head and the floor is tilting. Everything is going dark. I can't see!

No! she wanted to cry. It can't be. This is a nightmare. It can't be real!

She opened her mouth but no words came. The darkness swirled and drifted around her like a fog and from the vast void above her head came the echoes of John's voice,

'... *mine, Rachel. Mine and Rosemary's ...*'

She heard the shattering of a glass but it was a million miles away. Her knees trembled and buckled beneath her. She wanted Dan and his strength. She wanted him to tell her it would be all right.

'Dan?' she whispered then crumpled into merciful oblivion at John's feet.

TEN

The floor was no longer rocking beneath Rachel's feet and the ceiling above her head ceased to shift and sway. She was lying on the settee, now, with John kneeling beside her, his face tense and grey. Vaguely from the mists she remembered.

Anne was John's child—his and Rosemary's. Rachel wanted it to have been a mistake, a sad, sick joke but she knew it was neither. She tried to struggle to her feet but a wave of nausea washed over and she lay back again, limp and defeated, closing her eyes against her husband's anxious face, shutting out the truth. She wanted to scream protest, to hurt as she had been hurt but she was no longer in command of her mind or her body.

'Tell me?' she whispered.

Tell me that none of this is happening, her eyes begged mutely.

Grasping her hand, John held it to his cheek.

'I'm sorry, Rachel. I tried to keep it from you,' he groaned. 'God knows, I tried.'

It was true, then, she acknowledged dully, snatching her hand away. Her face crumpled and she wanted to be sick.

'Here. Drink this.'

She felt her head being raised, a glass against her lips. Pushing away his hands, Rachel forced herself into a sitting position.

'Why?' she whispered. '*Why?*'

John took a deep breath.

'Try to understand?' he jerked. 'Hear me out?'

Mutely she nodded, her eyes downcast. Her mouth was dry, her heart pounding in her throat. She knew when it all happened. The time in Manchester so long ago, when finally she accepted that she could never have a child. She had hugged her grief around her and shut John out.

'It was when I was driving, Rachel. I was on the Glasgow run. I gave her a lift—Rosemary, I mean. She was a student nurse and pretty hard up. She wanted to get to her sister's in Yorkshire. The lifts got to be a regular thing. I started to look forward to seeing her.'

'All those years, and I never knew.'

'Do you think I didn't want to tell you?' he gasped. 'Can you believe that sometimes I was desperate to bring it all into the open?'

'Then why didn't you?' Rachel demanded. Her voice was harsh now, reflecting the hurt that coursed through her.

'How could I tell you? There are some things that don't bear telling. To have got it off my chest would have been easy—the coward's way out. I had been an almighty fool and I knew I had to live with what I'd done—try to salvage something out of the awful mess.'

'What about Rosemary?' Rachel insisted. The pain inside her was almost unbearable yet still she had to know.

'Yes, I hurt her, too.' His voice was contrite. 'She didn't know I was married until it was too late. She asked me then if I loved you and I told her I did.'

He walked to the window and stood with his back to her, staring rigidly ahead.

'Hell! Do you think I was proud of myself, Rachel? Don't you think I was sick to my stomach, worrying about it all?'

'So you got Rosemary into the Home in Manchester?'

'No! It wasn't like that. I went to see the vicar, first —told him about it.'

'He knew? All the time Mr Whitaker knew? You arranged everything between you!' she gasped.

'No! You've got it wrong! I asked him for help—I didn't know where to turn. What he tried to do was what he sincerely thought would be best for everybody.'

'And Rosemary agreed? Dear God, how she must have suffered, knowing I had got her child.'

'But don't you see, she *didn't* know—not until yesterday. She had no idea who had adopted her baby, not until Sylvia Carson told her.'

'But Sylvia Carson denied all knowledge of Rosemary.'

'She would, wouldn't she? They were close friends—still are, it seems.' He sighed bitterly. 'Oh, if only you had told me you'd been there, Rachel...'

In a voice that was little more than a choked whisper Rachel asked,

'How did you know all this?'

'Sylvia Carson phoned Rosemary after you had left her house. It seems Sylvia thought that sooner or later you were going to find Rosemary so she decided to warn her.'

'And Rosemary got in touch with you, John? How did she know where to find you?' Rachel accused.

'Rosemary didn't know where I was,' John said wearily. 'She rang the number you had left with Mrs Carson.

She couldn't have known I would answer the phone. I had come home, you see, in case there was anything I could do to help. You were out, looking for Anne...'

He stopped, his face haggard, his voice dull with resignation.

'Rosemary phoned about an hour before you got back Rachel. She recognized my voice and broke down. I knew after that I would have to tell you everything—all I had kept back over the years...'

Rachel covered her face with her hands. Stupid fool that she was. She had blundered in blindly and left nothing but heartbreak behind her. Sick with remorse she whispered,

'What have I done? What's to be the end of it?'

She wanted to suffer. She wanted to be blamed for not heeding John's advice; she wanted him to rant at her for forcing everything into the open when it could have lain quiet forever. Instead he said,

'I'm sorry, Rachel. I hurt Rosemary and now I am hurting you. Well, if it gives you satisfaction, believe me I've paid for it—every single day of my life!'

Rachel closed her eyes and leaned back her head. She wanted to run away from the nightmare but her body was numb and useless and anyway she had to share the guilt, if guilt there was. Once, she had shut John out, refusing to acknowledge any other unhappiness save her own, denying him her love.

I drove him to Rosemary, Rachel thought, dully. John too was unhappy and lonely. Rosemary cared, and that was all that mattered. Dan cared when *I* was unhappy. Last night I needed Dan—it was so very easy. I didn't stop to think.

'Dear heaven,' she sighed. 'What a mess.'

Her voice broke and she bit hard on her lip. Not once, Rachel admitted, had John tried to implicate her. He had shouldered the responsibility and now he accepted all the blame. Suddenly, all shock and bewilderment drained away, leaving behind it a strange void.

'Rachel,' John urged, 'try to forgive me? Try to understand?'

I am trying to understand, she thought. You worked yourself to a near-standstill, drove yourself unmercifully. I thought it was blinkered ambition but it was really your way of trying to make atonement. But why weren't you able to tell me about it? Had we drifted so very far apart? She said,

'Is that why we left Manchester so suddenly?'

'Yes,' he acknowledged quietly. 'I thought it would be best if we tried to make a fresh start, but I soon found I couldn't leave my conscience behind me.'

Rachel cried then; sobs that shook her body and tore open her heart.

'Rachel—please don't? I know I've hurt you badly and if you walk out on me it'll only be what I deserve. But couldn't you at least try to understand?'

He stood there desolate, wanting to gather her to him yet knowing he dare not touch her.

She shook her head helplessly as the words she wanted to say avoided her. How could she explain to him that her anguish was not only for herself but for Rosemary, too; for a girl who had loved him and lost everything; for a woman who had just learned that her long-ago lover's wife had reared the child of that star-crossed union.

'Poor Rosemary,' Rachel said, eventually. 'What must

she be suffering, now? Can I do anything that might help?'

'You can meet her, Rachel. She asked that.'

'She wants to see *me*?'

'Only you, Rachel,' he nodded. 'Not me nor Anne. She asked especially that Anne should not be told anything about all this. Well?' he pleaded when Rachel remained silent. 'Will you meet her? Knowing what you know now, can you bring yourself to do it?'

For a moment Rachel was unable to speak, then through lips stiff with apprehension she jerked,

'All right, I'll do as she asks—I owe her that much. How can I get in touch with her?'

'You can't. She wouldn't give me her phone number. She asked that you get in touch with Mrs Carson in Manchester. She said Sylvia would arrange it. Will you do that, Rachel?'

A little less than an hour ago, Rachel thought, she would have given a great deal to meet Rosemary, but now she was unsure and apprehensive. How would such a meeting turn out?

Then she drew sharply on her breath.

'Yes,' she nodded. 'All right.'

Did she really, she thought sadly, have any choice?

Rachel looked at her watch yet again. She had travelled to York by train, realizing she was in no fit state to drive. She felt desperately alone. She wanted Dan's support but Rosemary was adamant, Sylvia Carson had told her over the phone. Three o'clock in the lounge of the hotel near the station—just the two of them.

Rachel's stay in York would be brief. She was to

return on the five o'clock train out and that gave her less than two hours in which to talk to Rosemary. She tried to look at it sensibly. Two hours that might fleet away in minutes could also stretch into a small lifetime. Looking about her, Rachel marvelled at the incredible normality of the scene. Women having tea and a gossip with friends before returning to their homes with their Wednesday shopping.

Will my life ever be normal again, Rachel wondered. Will things ever be the same? Since John's bombshell, there had been a kind of forced calm over the house, a calm so brittle that each of them knew it would take so little to shatter it. She was still numb yet was strangely glad of it. Soon, Rachel knew, she would have to face up to reality but not yet—not just yet...

What is Dan doing? she pondered, wishing yet again that he could be near her. Never had she needed his strength so much. She had decided against ringing him, knowing too well that to have heard his voice might be more than she could take in her present mood. Instead, she had sent him a letter, saying only that Rosemary had been found and begging that he should wait until she could contact him, and that John was home.

Please try to understand? she had written. *I will explain everything to you as soon as I can.*

Rachel shifted uneasily in her chair, determinedly trying to push all thoughts of Dan Steele from her mind.

Twelve minutes to three.

Supposing Rosemary didn't come or that they had got the time wrong and she had been and gone?

Then suddenly she was standing there, hesitant in the doorway. Rachel knew her at once. At a distance she seemed little changed from the girl in the snapshot save that her hair was now short and not so bright. Her legs heavy, Rachel rose to her feet and lifted her hand.

'Please,' she prayed silently, 'let everything be all right?'

Her mouth was dry and every pulse in her body throbbed dully. She wanted to smile, to say the words of welcome she had so carefully thought out, but she stood unspeaking.

Rosemary slowly walked nearer.

'Mrs Parker?' she whispered and Rachel inclined her head. 'Thank you for coming,' she choked.

For a moment the two women stood wary and embarrassed.

'Shall I serve you now, dear?'

'Oh, yes please,' Rachel nodded, grateful beyond measure to the waitress for her timely appearance.

'Tea and cakes, then,' the little woman chirped, blissfully unconcerned.

'Please,' Rachel said then took a deep breath as Rosemary sat down and arranged her shopping around her, eyes downcast. She had about her the stamp of a countrywoman. On her hand was a wedding ring.

'I don't know your name,' Rachel hazarded. 'Mrs . . . ?'

'Call me Rosemary, will you? It's best that way,' came the trembling reply.

Yes, Rachel thought dully; names can be traced.

'You live in York?' she ventured, trying to break through the uneasy silence.

'Twenty miles away—we have a farm. I come into town most Wednesdays, though.'

She ran her tongue round her lips and immediately Rachel felt compassion for her.

This is the woman my husband had an affair with,

she thought. She had his child and I should not care at all about her. But I do care because I am certain that at this moment, all she can think is that *I* am the woman who took that child. I am the woman who won, hands down.

'There we are, ladies.'

A tray was placed on the low table between them. Nervously Rachel picked up the teapot then replaced it with a thud, her hand jerking uncontrollably. Desperately she lifted her eyes to meet Rosemary's.

Help me? they begged. *Meet me half way?*

'Shall I pour?' Rosemary asked, softly.

'Please.'

Rachel let go a shuddering breath. The ice was broken. Surely now the worst was over?

Eyes downcast, Rosemary passed the tea, her hand unsteady.

'I don't really know why I asked you to meet me, Mrs Parker. Thank you for coming all this way.'

Rachel remained silent as with a visible effort the other woman lifted her head.

'I think I wouldn't have asked it if I hadn't found out about—'

'That it was John and I who adopted your baby?' Rachel prompted, gently.

'Yes. You see, when Sylvia phoned me—when I first realized the whole truth—I was very bitter. I felt cheated and betrayed but then I calmed down a bit. I phoned you at the number you left with Sylvia. I wanted to ask you to drop the whole thing—tell you I had suffered enough.'

'But John answered the phone instead,' Rachel whispered. 'I'm so sorry about that.'

'It was a shock—even after all the years...'

'I know how you felt, truly I do,' Rachel nodded sympathetically. 'I didn't know that John was Anne's father. It shocked me too, but then I began to realize it must have been pretty bad for him—having to hurt you and keep it from me. But mostly I was sorry for you, Rosemary—finding out who had got your little girl.'

'You really mean that?'

'Yes, I do. Oh, it's pretty bad to know you'll never have a child, but to have had one and be forced to give it up—well, I don't think I could have stood that...'

Her voice trailed away and she looked down at her clenched fingers.

'If it is any comfort to you, Rosemary, I love Anne with all my heart. That's why I tried to find you. Anne had to know that her other mother was a good person.'

'But you've since found out about me and John. Has it made you change your mind?' Rosemary whispered. 'Do you blame me—condemn me—for what happened between us, because if you do, remember I have paid...'

'No,' Rachel retorted, her voice thick with emotion. 'Nothing has changed and anyway, who am I to judge? Wasn't it partly my fault? I couldn't have a child so I made John suffer, too. He turned to you...'

There was a small, awkward silence then Rosemary said,

'I think I asked you to meet me because I wanted to know what you were like, Mrs Parker. I had to meet the woman who got my baby.'

'And now that you've met me?'

'I feel a little better about everything.' She gave a sad smile. 'Does Anne know anything of this?'

'No, I haven't told her and it's been the hardest thing I've ever done. I wanted to shout, "We've found your other mother, Anne. She lives in York and soon you'll be able to meet her".'

'You really were willing for us to meet? You didn't resent her wanting to know me?'

'No, why should I? My only feelings towards you were gratitude—always. Oh, please, couldn't you meet Anne?' Rachel urged. 'I know it's a lot to ask, but she does so need to see you.'

'No!' Rosemary's cup clattered to the table. 'You can't know what you are asking! See, I'll show you something ...'

She fumbled in her handbag, her fingers trembling, and brought out an envelope.

'That's all I ever had of my baby—that, and a memory. Oh, I'm happily married now and we have two wonderful sons, but there hasn't been a day I haven't wondered about Anne—worried about her—sent her my love ...'

Her face crumpled into tears.

'Go on,' she choked. 'Look at it.'

Inside the envelope was a narrow strip of plastic. Rachel recognized it at once; a birth-tag placed round the wrist or ankle of a newly-born child—a sentimental treasure. The one in her hand read,

Baby Jones. 2.10 a.m. 7/9/56.

Matron McIver had written it then recorded it in her baby-book.

'Oh, my dear.' Rachel lifted her eyes to Rosemary's. 'I didn't realize. I didn't know that—'

'That it could hurt like it was only yesterday I left Anne at that Home in Manchester?' She shook her head despairingly.

'Oh, no. You never quite get over it, Mrs Parker, so don't ask me to meet Anne—please? Don't rub salt in?'

With determination she mopped her eyes then took a gulp of tea.

'I'm sorry. I didn't mean to cry. Usually, I'm very good at keeping a hold of myself,' she whispered. 'I've had to, for my husband's sake. He doesn't know about Anne, you see. There are things it is best not to tell.'

'Yes, John said that,' Rachel breathed.

She returned the identity-tag to its envelope and handed it back.

'But will you tell me one thing, Rosemary? I ask it most humbly, believe me. Do you love John, still?'

Rosemary shook her head.

'No,' she replied. 'Not any more. I sometimes have difficulty even in remembering what he looked like.'

'But you did love him—once?'

'Yes, I loved him, but does it matter now?'

'To me it does, Rosemary. You see, I've often thanked God for giving me Anne and I've always prayed, "I don't know who her parents were, but let them have loved each other? Please let Anne have been a child of love?"'

Unable to continue she closed her eyes then gently whispered,

'Thank you for that, Rosemary...'

She opened her purse and laid a pound note on the table for the waitress to find then pushing back her chair and holding out her hand she said,

'I'll go now. I know you've had about as much as you can take. Goodbye, Rosemary. Thank you for everything and if by finding you I've caused you to be hurt in any way, please forgive me?'

Sadly she turned away.

'Mrs Parker?'

'Yes?' Rachel spun round.

'Tomorrow—I've got to come into town again. I'll see Anne here, at eleven o'clock.' The words came out in a desperate rush as though they must be said quickly, or not at all. 'Can she make it, do you think?'

'Yes. Oh, yes!' Rachel breathed.

'There's just one thing. I don't want to meet—I mean, Anne and I must be alone—just the two of us. Will you agree to that, Mrs Parker. Will you trust me?'

ELEVEN

Rachel stared fixedly at row upon row of parked cars and sighed dramatically. It caused her husband to raise his head from the inside of the bonnet where he had been needlessly tinkering. Closing it down and wiping his hands he said,

'Why don't you have a look around? York's an interesting old place. Better than sitting here, waiting and fretting, uh?'

'No,' Rachel snapped, then,

'Sorry. It's just that I'm a bit on edge and I'd really rather not. I want to be here when Anne gets back.'

'But she's only been gone an hour.'

'I know,' Rachel shrugged.

But why try to explain? To John the meeting between Anne and Rosemary was something to be over and done with as quickly and calmly as possible. But could he not realize that to their daughter it was a red-letter day? Ever since she had learned of her meeting with Rosemary, Anne's delight had bubbled over. She had worried about what to wear, tried her hair this way and that, fretted every mile of the journey north that they would be late.

'Well,' she laughed as she waved them good-bye, her cheeks flushed, her eyes bright with excitement, 'wish me luck?'

Her feet had danced impatiently across the car park

and towards the hotel where Rosemary would be waiting.

Rachel's heart thudded dully. She couldn't bear it, she thought, if Anne got hurt in any way. Not that Rosemary would knowingly upset her, but what if the two of them were to become emotionally involved? What would be the outcome if their parting was sad and tearful? What new heartbreak might be born?

I was so triumphant when Rosemary changed her mind so suddenly about meeting Anne, Rachel thought, but now I am desperately afraid.

John drummed his fingers on the driving wheel.

'Do you suppose they'll have lunch together?' he asked.

'I don't know,' Rachel returned absently, 'but there's coffee and sandwiches in the boot if you want any.'

John shook his head.

'No—thanks all the same.'

Oh, we are so polite, Rachel thought despairingly. For Anne's sake we are putting on a front when all the time since John told me, it has been like sitting on a powder-keg, waiting and wondering, trying to pretend that the day of reckoning can be put off indefinitely.

John had been wary—careful, almost—not to mention Rosemary's name again, skilfully sidestepping any of Anne's chance remarks that might start the whole thing up once more. It seemed as if both he and Rachel were playing for time, each afraid to take the initiative and say,

'Look, we've got to talk it out. We can't go on forever with this thing between us.'

But they had not done that because for their own private reasons, neither had wanted—or dared—to. John had shouldered the blame, Rachel thought uneasily but now to a lesser degree, she too was guilty. Like John, she had sought comfort. She had wanted to feel needed and cherished. It was natural to turn to Dan, she reasoned. Just, whispered her nagging conscience, as John once turned to Rosemary.

Suddenly she longed for the safeness of Dan Steele's presence. Oh Dan, Rachel sighed inside her, what did we do? Where is it all to end? Was it really only three days since she had lain in his arms? It seemed so far away—part of another lifetime. Now, she ached to hear his voice yet dare not allow herself even to lift the phone.

In a way she was glad that Dan had not got in touch with her yet all the while strangely sad about it. She was, she supposed, still in a state of deep emotional shock. It was as if she had shut down all feeling, unwilling to face up to the decision that soon she knew she must make.

John betrayed me, her subconscious insisted, and all those years he deceived me. But now I have betrayed John. Could two wrongs make up one right? Did each cancel out the other? Did she want them to?

She sighed impatiently. She was tired and drained emotionally. She had told Anne that Rosemary was found, painstakingly chosing her words, being careful not to mention anything of John's frightening admission. Anne must never know about that.

'Who's a clever old Mum, then?' Anne teased, her happiness a joy to see. 'Or was it the private eye? Was it your Mr Steele who found her?'

'Yes,' Rachel prevaricated, unable to look into John's apprehensive face, 'that's it. Anyway, we'll all have to be up bright and early in the morning. We've got to be there by eleven. Dad's going to drive us up.'

She explained to Anne about the meeting and how it would be best that she and Rosemary should be alone. Rachel had nearly choked on her glib deceit, grateful that Anne had been too excited to ask too many questions and had been easily satisfied.

Rachel looked again at her watch.

'What can they be talking about?' she said, half to herself as if she didn't expect an answer.

Would Anne be chattering happily away? Would Rosemary be talking about her sons—Anne's half-brothers—and the farm they lived on? Or would they, maybe, be sitting there distressed, wanting never to part?

Unable to bear the waiting any longer, Rachel thrust open the car door.

'What is it?' John jerked. 'Now, don't do anything foolish ...'

'I'm not. I'm going to get the coffee.'

She held out her hand for the boot-key and at once stopped in her tracks, instinct jerking her head upwards.

Anne was walking towards them. Her steps were slow and she glanced about her absently as if looking for the car. The buoyancy was gone from her walk, her shoulders drooped.

'Oh, no!' Rachel gasped.

Something was wrong.

'Anne's back,' she whispered, 'and something is wrong, I know it!'

In an instant, John was at Rachel's side. His hand reached for hers. It was cold as her own but it gave her comfort.

Anne saw them standing there and gave a brief smile.

'Hullo, parents,' she said.

Her voice was flippant, her face pale. She opened the car door and flopped down in the back seat then leaned back her head and closed her eyes.

'Leave her,' John mouthed to Rachel as they got into the car. Briefly their eyes met, his anxious, hers wide with apprehension. Unspeaking, John drove from the car park then gently eased his way into the slow-moving traffic. Rachel sat numb, seeing nothing. The quaint, ages-old city held no fascination for her as she watched Anne through the rear-view mirror, wanting to reach out to her yet not even daring to speak. Then suddenly John reached for a road map and tossing it on to the back seat beside Anne said,

'All right then—let's see how good you are at navigating. I want Leeds and the M1—Okay?'

His matter-of-fact voice jolted Anne's eyes open.

'Okay!' she confirmed, accepting the challenge, unfolding the map.

'Might even let you do a spot of driving on the motorway. Like that, uh?'

'Yes. Oh, yes!'

Rachel opened her mouth to protest that John's car was far too powerful for Anne to handle but at least the offer had served to shake the girl from the despondency that seemed to wrap her round.

Again Rachel sought John's eyes in the mirror.

Keep calm, he seemed to be saying. *Take it easy. She'll tell us, in her own time.*

'Traffic lights ahead. Stay in this lane for a left-turn,' Anne's voice came confidently.

Rachel sighed with relief. The outburst she was inwardly dreading had been avoided. She had to acknowledge that John had handled it beautifully. Gratefully, she settled down in her seat to wait.

They were speeding south on the motorway before Anne said,
'Well, go on—ask me.'
'All right. I'm asking,' her father quipped.
Anne took a breath, let it go dramatically then said,
'It was a flop—an all-time flop! I got myself so worked-up about it. I worried for years about my other mother and when I meet her it's a non-event. I've just met my mother and it was like having coffee with a stranger! It was as if—' she paused, searching for the right words —'as if I had gone into a crowded café and said to some woman, "Do you mind if I share your table?" and we'd got to chatting together ...'
'A stranger!' Rachel gasped. 'What do you mean?'
'I mean that she was pleasant and charming. She put me at my ease straight away and we talked about everything under the sun except that she was my mother and we were meeting for the first time!'
'And there was no emotion—no sort of—'
'There was *nothing*, Mum,' Anne whispered, her voice faintly disbelieving. 'Oh, I honestly didn't know what would happen, but I expected something more. Rosemary was just nice to me and kind—yes, that's it—she was *kind*, like I was the daughter of one of her friends. It was just out of this world.'
Shaking her head with disbelief she continued.
'She was somebody else's mother, not mine. Crazy, isn't it? We shook hands and said good-bye and she

gave me a little kiss on my cheek. Oh, heavens—talk about an anti-climax!'

Rachel closed her eyes. There was a sob of blessed relief in her throat but she choked it back.

'So it's going to be all right, Anne?' she whispered. 'Your mother *is* a nice person; she's not a tart, then?'

'Rosemary was sweet and my mother is a wonderful person. My mother is called Rachel and I am Anne Parker. Truth known, I've been Anne Parker all my life and if you know how sorry I am for being such a selfish little fool and how much I love you both right now—'

Her voice trembled and she blew her nose noisily then said with forced cheerfulness,

'Ah, well, that's my other mother taken care of. Now, I suppose, it's all a question of finding my other father.'

'*What?*'

Rachel flung round in her seat, her eyes wide with apprehension.

'Anne! Are you mad? You *can't* be serious?'

There was a muffled giggle and John's hands relaxed on the wheel as Anne said,

'Oh, Mum, I was just joking. Of course I don't want to find my real father!'

'Then don't ever say such a thing again! It was bad enough finding—'

Rachel dropped her eyes to her lap, unable to meet John's eyes.

'Mum—I've told you—it was a joke. Forget it.'

But John, it seemed, could not.

'Have you ever wondered about your father, Anne?'

He stared straight ahead and Rachel wanted to scream,

'No! Stop it! Let it lay...'

But she sat stock still in her seat, twisting and untwisting her fingers.

'My *real* father?' Anne pondered. 'No, Dad, I can't say I have, come to think of it,' she replied, her voice faintly disbelieving. 'You see, to me you always were my real father.'

'What do you mean?' Rachel whispered.

'Now don't get me wrong, Mum,' Anne puckered up her forehead, 'but somehow Dad always behaved like a real father. You know, if I got in late at night he would stand there bellowing, demanding to know where I had been and not believing me when I told him the truth. And he played merry hell, just like all the other dads did, when I'd had a bad school report. He never once,' she whispered, her eyes downcast, 'told me I was special or hand-picked or anything like that. He treated me as if I *was* his daughter...'

She leaned over the seat and placed her hand on Rachel's shoulder,

'Please don't be hurt, love. I know I'm making a mess of this, but I must say it. I wish, Mum, that you hadn't made a thing about my being adopted. I wish you'd just told me and then said, "But there's nothing special about you. You're Anne Vanessa Parker, that's all..."'

For a moment Rachel was too shocked and relieved to speak then slowly as she realized the danger was past, that Anne really had been teasing, she said,

'Ooh! You little madam! And the times I could have cheerfully slapped your bottom and didn't!'

'You should have, Mum,' Anne retorted soberly. 'Oh, but you should have!'

Then she turned to John and placing a kiss on his

cheek she said,

'So all in all, if you don't mind, that is, I think I'll keep you, bad temper and all. Come to think of it, I could have a done whole lot worse!'

John said,

'Stop it—you're distracting the driver.'

Then he grinned.

'Still want to get a bit of motorway driving in? Shall I pull in at the next service station?'

'No thanks Dad. Not this time. Just keep her going, will you. I want to get back home as quickly as you like. I've got to see Graham. I want to tell him I'll marry him, if he's fool enough to still want me!'

For the rest of the journey, little was said and Rachel stared unseeing ahead. Despite herself, she felt a flood of pity for her husband. How dreadful that he had had to joke about such a thing; how sickening that he had not once over the years been able to stand tall and proclaim,

'This is Anne, my beautiful daughter! Look at her, everyone—she's mine!'

And he could never take Anne's face gently in his hands and say,

'Yes, you are my child. Once, briefly, I loved and you came with that love. You were my daughter and I couldn't let you go. I have endured twenty years of misery, knowing that.'

Anne would never know unless she, Rachel, were to say,

'He *is* your real father, Anne. All those years I did not know. He deceived me and I cannot find it in my heart to forgive him.'

What would happen to Anne's newly-bright world if she were to say that, Rachel pondered, a sick feeling gnawing at the pit of her stomach. And what of Rosemary who had suffered most of all? Vaguely uneasy, Rachel lived again the events of the last two days. She thought of Rosemary as two persons; the one she had met yesterday and the one who today had entertained Anne to coffee and polite chat. Yesterday's Rosemary had been a tragic figure, a woman who could not forget, who begged not to be asked to meet her daughter. Then suddenly and inexplicably she had agreed to the meeting—just she and Anne, alone. *Alone.* There, if anywhere, lay the key to it all. Alone, Rosemary of today could put on an act, manage to convince Anne that in twenty years memories grow dim and wounds can heal, that her baby was a vague remembrance.

How was it possible to do such a thing? Rachel marvelled. How could Rosemary have found the strength? It was near-unbelievable that deliberately she could have so completely and finally cut the ties that bound them.

Oh Rosemary, Rachel's heart yearned. What in my stupidity have I done to you?

'Quite a post,' John said as he scooped up the mail from behind the door and sorted quickly through it. Then he stopped and stared hard at a pale blue envelope.

'For you,' he jerked.

The letter was postmarked *York. 5.15 p.m.* and Rachel knew, as John did, that it was from Rosemary. She probably thought I would get it this morning before we left, Rachel thought, but we set out early, before the postman called.

As if he knew she wanted to be alone to read it, John said,

'Think I'll make a cup of tea. Want one?'

Rachel nodded absently, her fingers unsteady as she tore open the envelope. There was no letter inside, just a strip of plastic wrapped inside a sheet of notepaper, bearing the words,

Baby Jones—2.10 a.m.—7/9/56.

A gasp tore straight from Rachel's heart and she heard again Rosemary's whispered words,

'That's all I ever had of my little girl...'

Gently Rachel closed her fingers round it, her heart pounding with pain.

She sent me this because she wanted me to understand, Rachel thought. I was right. Rosemary treated Anne like a stranger today because she knew it was the only thing to do. She cut the last precious link between them and she did it deliberately, for Anne's sake. The little tag in Rachel's hand confirmed it. She could almost hear Rosemary's voice pleading softly,

'Anne is all yours, now. I surrender her completely. Love her for me—always?'

'Oh, Rosemary,' Rachel whispered, a love washing over her that she had never thought possible. 'Thank you. Thank you with all my heart.'

TWELVE

Rachel slipped Rosemary's envelope carefully inside her handbag. Her heart still pounded with compassion and unshed tears ached in a tight little knot in her throat. Like a homing bird she made for the summer-room and its green tranquillity. She hoped John would not follow her. She was afraid that soon he might want to talk about the Manchester affair and first, Rachel knew, she had to be quite sure of her own feelings.

At least, she thought, Anne's problems are settled. She is content now and all is right with her world. Soon, she and Graham will be married and she will no longer need me.

Rachel tried to imagine the wedding day of Dan's daughter. How had she felt, with parents who had parted? Had it clouded her happiness that day? But Dan and his former wife had put a brave face on it.

'Elaine and I acted in a very civilized manner...'

Civilized. What an unfeeling word it was, Rachel pondered. Will John and I be like that at Anne's wedding? Will we too be acting a part, pretending that the Manchester affair never happened, or will it all have to come into the open? Before this strange day is over, will I have decided to leave John? Has he guessed about Dan Steele and me? Is that why he is so quiet, so withdrawn. Is he trying to make things easy for me?

But could she, Rachel ruthlessly demanded of herself, walk out on twenty-five years of marriage? Could she truly bring herself to say,

I am leaving you, John. I have fallen in love with another man. There is nothing, now, to keep me here and he needs me more than you need me. He and I have been lovers. I am as guilty as you, John, and with much less cause.

Rachel closed her eyes wearily. John had been faced with such a decision nearly twenty years ago. When Rosemary had told him about the baby, he had had to choose—his wife who no longer seemed to want him or the girl who had given him love without question and the promise of the child he so desperately desired.

And he chose me, Rachel thought dully. Even though I had shut him out of my heart, denied him the comfort of my body, still he would not leave me. What a terrible decision John had had to make. And when it was all over, when Anne was theirs, how he must have suffered, knowing he had hurt the mother of his child and deceived the woman who was his wife.

'I had been a fool. I alone had to live with it...'

For twenty years he had lived with it and paid for it and was prepared to go on paying.

Now it is all up to me, Rachel thought wildly. John needs my forgiveness yet I too am guilty. Now it was she who had acted unwisely, she conceded, and just as John had done all those years ago, she too knew that she could not cleanse her soul by confession. She could not thrust the burden onto John. John had suffered enough.

And what of Rosemary's suffering and sacrifice? Rosemary had lost everything. Even now she must hug her secret to her. What had she said?

'My husband doesn't know about Anne. There are things it is best not to tell...'

John knew that, too, Rachel pondered. He carried his secret within himself because to have told it all would have achieved nothing save to ease the burden from him to me.

How then could she leave, Rachel asked herself? How could she take Rosemary's sacrifice and make it as nothing? Rosemary had sent the pathetic little identity-tag and in doing so had given up her child for all time. Could she then betray Rosemary, Rachel pondered—the girl from Morvedd who had given her so much? Could she walk out on her marriage, wrecking all they had built up over the precarious years? Could she cause Anne unhappiness? Didn't Anne's happiness count for most? Rosemary had known that many years ago when she had left her little girl with Matron McIver.

Can we always, Rachel thought, take what we want? And if we do, is it right to make someone else pay for it?

'There hasn't been a day I haven't wondered about Anne—worried about her—sent her my love...'

Rosemary's words came back mistily to Rachel. Rosemary who had found her daughter only to treat her with kindness then send her back to the woman who had become her mother. Wasn't there something to be learned from that, Rachel mused sadly or was she too blind and too selfish to recognize it? Did she want to recognize it? demanded her conscience.

Shaking her head impatiently, she gathered up her handbag and coat. Without further thought, she picked up the telephone extension and dialled a number.

'Dan? It's Rachel.'

'Darling! Where have you been? Why couldn't I contact you? What's been happening?'

His joy at hearing her voice was unmistakable.

'Listen Dan, I'm coming down now. I'll be with you in about half an hour—all right?'

'Sure, but let me pick you up?'

'No, I'll drive myself.'

She replaced the receiver then spun round instinctively. John was standing in the doorway, a tea-tray in his hands.

'The inquiry agent?' he asked, his voice low.

Rachel nodded. 'I'm going to see him,' she said.

'All right, but Rachel—'

He stopped, his eyes pleading.

'Yes, John?'

'Do you have to go?'

'Yes,' she replied gently. 'I have to go.'

'Okay, then I suppose I might as well go back to the depot. Maybe I can catch up on the work a bit...'

'When will you be back, John?'

'Oh, I don't know. Late, most likely. Miss T. can fix me something to eat from the canteen. When will *you* be back, Rachel?'

For just a moment she hesitated.

'I'm sorry. I don't know.'

John nodded and walked slowly from the room, head bent, as if he were afraid to look into her face and read what was in her eyes.

The front door banged and Rachel heard the revving of a car. Slowly she shrugged into her coat, then picking up her car keys, walked purposefully from the room. She knew now exactly what she would do and the decision once taken seemed like the lifting of a great weight from her shoulders.

Dan Steele was waiting impatiently. Hardly had Rachel closed his office door behind her than he gathered her into his arms.

'Darling,' he breathed, 'it's been an age. The times I nearly rang you ...'

Then he smiled and tilted her chin with his fingertip and kissed her, gently at first as if to satisfy himself she were real, then hungrily and urgently. Rachel sighed and relaxed in his arms, clinging to him as if she would never let him go.

'Rachel,' he whispered, 'I thought you would never come. Is everything all right, now? Have you seen Rosemary?'

'Yes, and everything is going to be fine.'

'Where was she? How did you manage it?'

'It was through Sylvia Carson,' Rachel replied, eyes downcast. She seemed strangely reluctant to discuss the matter, even with Dan. 'Sylvia lied to me. She knew all the time where she was. After I had left her house she phoned Rosemary and Rosemary got in touch with us, from somewhere near York.'

'Just like that? Then what?'

'Well—to cut a long story short, Rosemary and Anne met in York, this morning. It went off very well, I believe. Of course, Anne realizes it was a once-only meeting but she seems quite content, now.'

Rachel could not bring herself to look into Dan's face. She hated herself for her evasiveness. Dan deserved to know the whole truth. After all, had it not been for him, they might never have found Rosemary. She wanted to say,

'Rosemary was very upset about the whole thing. She begged not to be asked to meet Anne but she agreed in the end, and for Anne's sake she acted like a stranger towards her own child.'

And she owed it to Dan to tell him about John and Mr Whitaker and the anguish John had been forced to bear for so long.

'Ever since we got Anne he had to live with the knowledge that at any time I might find out about his affair with Rosemary. It must have been dreadful for him, never being able to acknowledge his own daughter. And it was all my fault. John couldn't cope with my blind grief. I shut him out—forced him into Rosemary's arms. He has suffered enough for what I did.'

But she knew she would never tell Dan the whole truth because she knew she had no right to betray either John or Rosemary. It was their secret, paid for with tears and unhappiness. It was theirs, alone. Already, Rachel suddenly realized, too many people had been hurt. Now there must be no more pain. She must take her cue from Rosemary and act as she had done. Rosemary had found the strength to cut the thread that bound her to Anne. Now she, Rachel, must do the same to Dan. That she could learn to love him with all her heart could not be gainsaid; that she was free to love him was another matter.

Dan smiled, unaware of the turmoil that raged inside Rachel. He said,

'Sit down, sweetheart. I'll make you some coffee, then we can talk. Are you staying?'

His eyes begged her to, then he smiled boyishly and switched on the kettle.

'Milky, isn't it and no sugar?'

'Yes please and Dan—I'm not staying.'

She saw his head jerk upwards, a wary expression flit across his face.

'But Rachel—'

'No Dan,' she said evenly, every word a dull pain 'I mean it. I came tonight to thank you for all you have done and to settle up.'

'*Settle up?*' Dan jerked, his mouth tight, his eyes narrow as if she were offering him Judas money. 'You want now to turn it into a business deal—is that it, Rachel?'

'That's the way it started out, Dan and that's the way it's got to end. And it must end, Dan. You and I both realize that if we are to be honest. It's got to stop before innocent people get hurt—people who have suffered enough already.'

'Like who?' Dan demanded, bluntly.

'Oh, it doesn't matter.'

She shook her head helplessly. She wanted to run to him, to feel his arms around her one last time, his cheek rough on hers but she held herself in check against him.

He was silent for a moment, his brow furrowed into a scowl, his mouth set tight. He looked, Rachel thought, exactly as he had done the night they met. There was a button missing still from his shirt and Rachel longed, just this once, to take a needle and thread from her handbag and sew it back on. Instead she whispered,

'What do I owe you, Dan?'

'Oh, call it a hundred quid,' he said, 'and I'd like a cheque, please.'

He sat quite still for a moment then when Rachel did not speak he said,

'It all seemed to be going for us, Rachel, and yet somehow I knew nothing would ever come of it,' he sighed, resignedly as Rachel bent her head over her cheque book. 'Even though we both seemed so right for each other—needed each other so much. But you're too decent, my darling.'

His words hit Rachel like a physical blow.

Oh, but I am not decent, she thought grimly. I cared only about myself and my sorrow. I drove John to another woman and when I decided to look for Anne's other mother, I didn't stop to think who I would be hurting in the process. And I let myself fall in love with you, Dan. I did what John once did and it was so good. Now, I must hurt you, too.

She signed the cheque shakily then passed it to him unspeaking. Briefly their hands touched and their eyes met then Dan rose to his feet and held out his hand. She knew he wouldn't plead with her—not stubborn Dan Steele.

'Good-bye, Rachel. It's been great knowing you.'

'Thanks for everything,' she whispered.

At the door she turned and tried to smile. Dan lifted his eyes and they were like those of a wounded animal; in his hand her cheque was crumpled into a ball. He said,

'If you ever need me, Rachel—if things don't work out—I'll be here. I'll always be here...'

She nodded, sadly.

'Good-bye, Dan.'

Blinded by tears, Rachel eased her car into the kerb at the top of the street where Dan lived. Her whole body ached as she fought back great sobs of agony. Stuffing her fist into her mouth she bit hard on her knuckles, the physical pain it caused giving her a grim kind of satisfaction.

'Oh, Dan,' she choked. 'What have I done to you?'

She hoped he would be able to forgive her, to realize in time that she had said good-bye to him in the only way she knew how. Their parting had had to be short and sharp with no explanations allowed. To have opened her heart to him would have been impossible. She had done as Rosemary had done and cloaked her real feelings in the certain sad knowledge that the means would justify the end. Now she hugged herself tightly, rocking to and fro in her misery, choking on her tears. Soon she would be all right. Soon, the pain would ease and she would mop her eyes, take a deep, steadying breath then drive away from the narrow street and out of Dan's life for all time. It was all she could do. She was allowed no choice. Their affair was over before it had had time to tarnish and spoil. Now, it would always remain bright, a little gem to treasure, to remember always, a brief, sweet interlude.

A patrolling policeman turned the corner and walked slowly down the deserted street towards her. The turmoil within her had spent itself, her muddled thoughts had cleared. Turning the ignition key, Rachel slid the car into gear and slipped gently away. She did not even allow herself a fleeting, backward glance.

Rachel parked her car beside John's then let herself quietly into Fair Oaks. No light shone from any window and the house was broodingly quiet. But for all that, she was glad John was back home. She didn't know what she would say to him or what he would ask of her, but still she was glad.

She found him sitting in the garden-room, his shoulders hunched, his eyes closed. It was evident he had neither seen nor heard her approach because when she stood behind him and laid her hands on his shoulders she felt a sudden jerking of his body.

'Rachel?' he whispered, his voice husky with disbelief.

'Yes John.'

She waited for him to ask her about Dan, but he did not.

'You came back?' he said. 'I didn't think—I didn't dare hope ...'

Oh, yes, she thought, I came back. It would have been easy for me to go to Dan. A little while ago, I might have done it, but not any more. I've learned so much, these last two days. I know now that two wrongs don't make a right and that already there has been too much unhappiness. The Manchester affair is over and it has been paid for. I must try to put it all behind me because neither of us has been wholly guilty or entirely innocent.

'What I'm trying to say,' John continued, 'is that I wouldn't have blamed you ...'

He reached for her hand and laid it to his cheek.

'Are you all right, Rachel? Does it hurt very much?' he whispered, turning to face her.

His tenderness and understanding brought a fresh rush of tears to her eyes. Unspeaking she nodded, her eyes imploring him to help her, not to ask her about Dan—not just yet ...

He said gently,

'Give it time, Rachel. Everything passes in time. Soon, it won't be so bad ...'

She sighed tremulously, grateful beyond belief for his kindness, his gentleness, and a small soft wave of peace washed over her.

Turning away from Rachel, John walked slowly to the open doorway and stood staring out at the dusky outlines of the garden. Head erect he said,

'Can we try again, Rachel? I know it won't be easy for you, but for Anne's sake, even if it is only until after the wedding, couldn't we try? I'd not make any demands or ask for anything you weren't willing to give me, but I don't think I can bear to live without you.'

His voice cracked with emotion and he stood very still, staring ahead at the blossom-scattered grass, waiting tensely for her reply.

Slowly she walked towards him and slipped her hand into his. For a moment they stood, shoulders touching, then as if by mutual consent they turned to face each other and in her eyes John saw gentleness and understanding. Only briefly he hesitated then with an exclamation of joy and relief he held out his arms.

'Rachel?' he pleaded.

She went to him slowly, shyly, and for a while they stood unspeaking and uncertain, knowing the way ahead would not be easy but each of them determined to try. Slowly Rachel felt the tension leave her body and sensed an answering response in his.

'Well?' she whispered and he heard the smile in her voice.

Huskily John said,

'I love you, Rachel.'

He said it as he used to say it in the Manchester days, and the words were sweet with hope.